For My Best Friend

Janice Vuler

Contents

1- The party.

It was a regular high school party at britanny's house, the queen bee of armadillo high. Britanny was dating the hottest guy,the eye candy, the football captain Zack Ryder who, ofcourse was my, Savannah orlove's best friend. Let me introduce myself, a normal 17 y/o teenager who has good grades,isn't popular , has like two best friends,one of them which happens to be Zack and riley. I haven't had a bunch of boyfriends, to be precise I have never had boyfriend, that's not a big of a deal but my best friends put in a lot of effort for finding me "the perfect one".

Back at the party,the whole school was there having a great time some of the people were wasted af, some were busy making out or hooking up and i was sitting all alone on the couch with my fruit punch watching people have the time of their life. I am an introvert though Zack forced me to come to this party so i had to. While i was there i heard screams,infact everyone did. Zack and britanny were screaming on the top of their lungs and that's when Zack said " I am breaking up with you , you cheat".

Britanny was in tears, her little wannabe followers were making her quiet n that's when Zack left the party, being a good friend i went after him to check what was up. Zack had a very bad temper but i knew how to calm him down . I asked him to sit down n that's when he spoke" Brittany kissed leo",zack's elder brother, he continued " they were making out on the couch while i went to get her punch, and this is the second time she is doing this and the only reason she gives me is that i don't pay enough attention to her and leo looks like me so she kissed him" i was furious i said "that bitch deserves to suffer" and hugged him.

Our hug usually is like for a second but this one was intense, like i could feel the pain he was going through and when i broke the hug, I stared into his deep blue eyes and felt nervous the way i was never before. We went home and he said he would text me the next day.

I went home and kept thinking about that eye contact and the intensity in his eyes soon i dozed off.

Part 2- Bitch alert!

✱ I will be adding POV'S of the characters at several points on the story*

.. The news of zack's breakup was buzz for the next few days in our school, all the girls who didn't get a chance with Zack coz of britanny were now drooling all over him. Many girls be it juniors or seniors they all approached Savannah, to get closer to Zack of course. Whereas, Brittany was the total social attention seeker now, she had been manipulating people and saying them that Zack was the one who cheated on her with Savannah , at first Savannah didn't seem to care neither did Zack, but then the picture of Zack and Savannah hugging after the party was leaked by one of Brittany's so called "wannabe followers" and it blew up.

Savannah had to face a lot of critcism after it whereas Zack's football teammates to criticized him for cheating. Savannah was basically bullied for something she didn't do. But Zack had a lot of nerve and he started hanging out with Savannah alot in school which reinforced the fact that Zack had completely moved on but while dating Brittany, he was used to all the fake rumours .

Britanny,on the other hand was still not done, she was still in the revenge mood as she always was very insecure about Savannah. She was still willing to get Zack back as all her reputation and popularity was because of Zack.

Savannah POV - I really didn't care about the shit britanny was up to the only fact i liked here that Zack was spending more time with me instead of his other group which ofcourse is good because we are best friends after all. ____

During the lunch break riley,Savannah and Zack were on one table and Britanny had been giving her the most evil stares it was sure she was upto something but Zack reassured Savannah that she won't do anything as she is harmless. That's when Britanny spilled the grape juice on Savannah, before Savannah could say something in her defence Zack stood up and lashed out on Britanny " That's enough! We had broken up over a month ago, get over it. It was cool till u spread rumours about me and Savannah because we knew that bitches like you can't do any better, but hurting Savannah on purpose is a big deal. If you don't back off this right second then i am going to leak your's and leo's making out photos, and i am sure you must have the brains now to stop with your plan".

The whole cafeteria was in shock , riley and Savannah were shook head to toe, Britanny cried and left the cafeteria thats when Zack turned to Savannah , smiled and whispered," I got your back anna." The lunchbreak was over and riley and Savannah were going to class and riley said ," So, Zack is pretty defensive for you,huh?" Savannah said ," Duh, we are best friends he did what was right" riley continued "best friends? Of please that's something a boyfriend would do, plus you were blushing so bad that my blusher would have failed if it competed with you." Savannah got awkward and said "i didn't blush." Riley said ,"oh please i always knew you had the hota for each but ut was just a best friend sugar coating layer on it" Savannah Chuckled and said ," hots for the guy whom i have seen wearing his sister's heels and makeup? Oh please i wont even let my aunt have the hots for him." Riley said ," sooner or later I will be proved right babe."

Savannah's POV- the day got over pretty quick, but what riley said was stuck in my mind, Zack was pretty defensive and did sound like a protective boyfriend but i never thought of him as a boyfriend ,maybe because we are too different and we have different worlds though we still are the best of friends, that's when i had this crazy thought of what would happen if we actually dated i loved everything about that guy he had the same qualities i would like to see in my boyfriend but was not sure.

Savannah slept and woke to Zack's text ," Hey,party at Greg's at 8 pm be ready i will pick you up;)." Savannah smiled a bit and got ready.

Let's see how this party changes the relationship between Zack and Savannah;)

Part 3 soon

Part 3- The Dare.

At Greg's party Zack and Savannah went together there was loud music, lots of food and ofc the hooking ups, that's when Greg announced "Wassup peeps! Rather than all the random hooking let's play a game of dares, it's just like truth and dares except we only give dares here. No one can change or say no to a dare. Cool?" The whole room shouted "Woohoo yes!!" Zack said "Savannah, don't be a buzzkill let's go it's just dares" Savannah said hesitantly," Ughokay."

Well this was not something new, The dares were just about kiss this girl or drink all the shots there, like any normal party would have, but Savannah hated dares as she thought they were illogical . That's when Greg shouted again," Sooooo, next dare is on Savannah, As your 'best friend' broke up with his girlfriend now you gotta have a full makeout session with Zack."

Woah. The whole room started cheering Savannah and Zack were awkward as hell they couldn't look into each other's eyes . Everyone started cheering *Zacannah* . Greg again said ," remember the rules u can't say no to this dare." Zack stood up and said," if she isn't comfortable i wont, we are best friends. You can't force us." Greg said," Bro it's my party you have to agree to the rules that i make, it is kinda how it works." Zack gave Savannah a look she said "okay" but she was a bit hesitant and that's when the kiss happened, people started recording or shouting "i knew they wouldn't be best friends for long" the girls who were head over heels for Zack were cursing Savannah for breaking the " Girl code 101". Savannah broke the kiss, and they looked into each other's eyes and pretended that nothing happenedOn the way home there was awkwardness between the two of them, Zack broke the silence and said ,"Hey it was just a dare we are still and always be best friends i dont care whatever rumours spread around." Savannah gave a little smile and said,"Ya ofcourse,sure." After that both of them went home

Savannah quickly went home and called riley who was sitting on a beach in Hawaii. (Well i forgot to mention she is awfully rich)Savannah called her up and explained everything not leaving out a single detail,"Riley? Where are you? Helllooooo?!" Riley was startled," ARE YOU FCKN KIDDING? JUST A WEEK AGO YOU WERE FRIENDZONING THAT GUY AND U HAD YOUR FIRST KISS WITH HIM?!" Savannah said," You need to calm down riles." Riley again screamed ," CALM DOWN?! I said u had the hots for each other, it feels so good to be proved right omggg yaaasssss!!!!!" She continued ," okay so will you date or something now? Please tell i am dying of curiosity babee." Savannah said in a light voice, "Actually we haven't talked about it....... But i will for sure tomorrow sure i guess idk i will you chill k bye!" And she hung up that's when riley said to herself ," she so loves him wow."

Next day at school Savannah went to Zack and he acted like nothing ever happened. Savannah said ," Hey do you wanna talk about the kiss earlier?" Zack continued, "Oh it was nothing for me don't make a big deal out of it it was just a kiss." Savannah was disappointed and she said ," Yeah, just a kiss, and mumbled," my first kiss was never that important okay." And left.

Savannah called riley and ranted "how can Zack Ryder be such a bitch?! My first kiss meant nothing to that asshole?? He was the one who was the most excited that when will i have my first kiss and he has a plain reaction when i actually get one?!! Okay I get it i never imagined him to be my first kiss but still he should have talked to me about it!" Riley said calmly," why are you getting so affected? He did the right thing by not bringing it up right?" Savannah said, 'Uhh maybe,like yes ofc no big deal, i gotta go now bye."

Savannah's POV - i couldn't stop thinking about the kiss i knew it was just a stupid dare and I should not be affected that much but i just kept thinking about it i couldn't sleep because of it it was going on and on and on like a replay and i couldn't stop myself from smiling at that point . I never looked at Zack that way atleast i thought i won't ever in my life but that party and date changed my whole 'buddy' opinion about him. I opened my Instagram and i stalked him, all the girls commented ,' so perfect ' , 'marry me' and i was kind of bugged that's when Zack texted and my face lit up and i hurriedly opened his text which said " bro i got a date this Sunday, and the girl is hottt, wish me luck!!"

Woah. Savannah was shocked she left the text on read and slept.

Has Savannah fallen for her best friend? Will she get jealous if she sees Zack and her date together? Keep reading to know!

Part 4- Zack's date

- -

Hey all! So i decided to bring a bit of change in the story. A friend of mine suggested to write this in the first person i.e Savannah, i put a lot of thought to it and it was turning out to be good that way you won't be comfues with many POV's . Thanks!!!

****

This week passed within a blink of an eye and i tried my best to avoid... I mean I didn't talk to Zack much, he was pretty excited about his date with a girl named Quinn Forester. Boy she was HOT. Zack didn't make too much effort to talk, neither did he notice me much . I don't know why i wanted him to notice me as it has never happened before, but I just wanted him to talk to me,even if he came to talk about why isn't apple called red if orange is called orange boy wtf is wrong with me. I never thought I'd be this dumb so that a guy could talk to me.

Well here i was lying on couch like a sloth bear still trying to take out the moment b/w me and Zack from my head, but my hormones just kept on imaging more intimate scenarios that could take place between us. This never happened with any guy before, i just kept on thinking this will pass and maybe it's just lust and i should let go of it and all, but that's when i heard a knock at my door , I didn't feel like getting up so mum opened that gate and shouted ," Anna! Zack is here.

WHATT!?!?! ZACK IS HERE!

Mum shouted,"come down fast anna!"

I couldn't go like this! I look like i haven't taken a bath since a week and what the heck was wrong with my hair?! Wait. Why am i so concerned what i would look like in front of my best friend? He isn't gonna kill me or judge me or lose the -000.1 interest he has in me right?

I still combed my hair and went down , I should have been prepared to see what was in front of me it was Zack and he was wearing a black leather jacket with a white Beatles shirt inside and black ripped jeans. He was carrying a bouquet of lillies (my favourite kind of flowers) and he smelled like a fresh summer breeze. Why does he look so perfect?! Wait he has lillies, has he come to ask me out? What ofc not or maybe yes?I mean yeah we kissed but does he like me? Ew my best friend can't like me. But he looks so perfect .Can i hug him atleast?

"Savannah? Are you there? Helloooooo wake upp." I came out of my fantasy world and was like ,"yeah yes, oh hey what brings you here? Are u alright? You look hot wow. FML did i just say that!?

Zack said, "calm down Sherlock, i know i look hot but I wont when i meet Quinn. QUINN. That name stuck in my head,even I haven't met her yet i already knew i hated her to death. I calmed down and said ,"wow she likes lillies too?" Zack said ,"I really don't know I assumed if u love lilles she would atleast like them."

Aww. He remembers i love lilles could he be cuter? Huh wait get out of here.

Why are you so lost today? Said Zack to which i replied,"me? Huh whaaat-tttt? U look lost okay, i look perfect if you don't leave soon u may lose your way hahahaaa." I knew Zack was confused as heck, he gave a smile and left l, i shut the door behind him.

Why didn't I get some sense of humour?

I called riley, the only person I wanted to talk to then, and told her everything , giving every detail how Zack looked ,how good he smelled and how my heart melted when he grinned. Riley didn't say a word during the whole convo and when i asked ," I have no clue what is wrong with me." Riley said," wrong? Aw babe no , it's just that you have fallen for Zack. Infact you are madly in love with him."

Wow. Those words hit me hard .

Riley wasn't wrong i really had fallen for him.

I couldn't help but smile but at the same time i knew it's not gonna work out.

I said to riley," But we can never be together, he would never like me, I mean look at me, I am not popular neither I am that pretty, i dont have the perfect 'thicc' figure i am just average." Riley said, "wow you so love him that you could have won an Oscar in self critcism and she laughed. "Riles! I am serious here, i dont want to fall for some or or like someone who doesn't like me back and has friendzoned me already, I don't wanna cry over a guy, why is it so hard? Can i just unlike him ?" Riley got irritated," ANNA HE IS A GUY NOT A FACEBOOK POST!" I said ,"I will try to stay away so that i start loving me best friend." Riley replied," too late you already do;)" and she cut the call.

This is the worst day of my life.

Savannah has fallen for her best friend. How is this going to affect their relationship? Will they date? Or drift?

Keep reading "Friends with benefits" to get know about this .

Until then byee.

part 5- The unprofessional spies

"So, what's your plan now?" Said riley, "plan? What plan?" I asked confused as heck. Riley stood up and looked at me with a dissapointed look and screamed," THE LOVE OF YOUR LIFE IS DOWN AT THE RESTURANT,HOLDING HANDS WITH SOME OTHER GIRL AND YOU WILL DO NOTHING? IS THAT WHAT U HAVE LEARNT?!"

WOAH I was startled, i had never seen riley in such a mood, apparently she was more into my love life than i would have ever been. "What do you think riles? What can i possibly do? He must be looking at her with his beautiful blue eyes and they would be talking about how pathetic it was to kiss me and maybe later he forgets about me and moves on with his life, he would marry that perfect Quinn and i would be left alone in this whole wide world with no boyfriend. I will be the grumpy old lady who is still a virgin at the age of 35, with a cat in a big gloomy house. Wait i dont wanna stay a virgin, do you think i should become a prostitute? Like they earn good but i dont have the body ughhh it's like i am two months pregnant already without having sex. My life is great isn't it?" I stopped to catch my breath and i have never seen riley staring at me so bad, its like i just said

Harry Potter is shit (she loves Harry Potter, and she would have married Draco Malfoy if he was real person) . I was like "don't stare at me like that please."

Riley took a break and continued, "How much do you love Zack? You literally just planned his wedding coz he was on a date! And you wanted to be a prostitute for a reason that is not even reality!!!"

Wow, i just recalled what i said. How can just a kiss affect me so much? Am i really that in love with Zack?

" We should spy on Zack and his date!!!" Riley exclaimed. I gave her the weirdest look and said ," that's so immature, i can't barge into his date and be like oh hey Zack, the love of my life, i just came here to spy on you because i am super jealous that you are on a date with someone else." Riley hit me on the head and said ," aw babe you are so naive, we will SPY on him which means he won't be able to see us, i have got the perfect outfits!" Is your best friend such a drama queen? coz mine is out of control.

"What are you waiting for?!" Riley screamed, I said ," is this the right thing to do? Like it's just feelings, maybe just a bit infatuation,or it's just lust you never know." Riley held my face in her hands and said," if you think about a guy all day and imagine your whole life just because he is on a date it's not infatuation,plus love is a wonderful feeling. You gotta accept you have fallen way too hard for him. He is yours and we should separate him from the hot stuff, QUINN. Are you ready anna?"

Was i ready? I mean he is my best friend it's just a bit spying which is wrong but it won't harm right?

I was hesitant, but i agreed to spy on Zack and Quinn. Riley got us our 'spying outfits' , we got changed and headed to the restaurant they both were in. It took us a while to figure out where they were coz it was filled with people. That's when I heard someone ordering ,"two slices of chicken dominater,white sause pasta with oregano and chicken without vegetables and a sprite would be convenient with it." That's Zack , of course it's him i know his order so well! No one else would order such a combo i guess i looked that way and saw Zack and Quinn sitting together and having a good laugh, boy i was jealous I WAS SO SO SO JEALOUS, I WANTED TO BE WITH ZACK!!! Riley poked me and said ," cool down sis, a little more jealousy and people could have a barbecue." She is sarcastic huh.

So we went near to their table and luckily we found a empty table near them. We tried our best so that Zack could not see us, we his behind the menu cards and i was constantly staring them they were cute together, i can't stop Zack from trying to date who he wanted that's when i thoughtWill he ever like me? I am not worth him that he hasn't noticed me all these years.

I was snapped out if my imagination and that's when riley said," let's go near them i am sure you want to hear what they are talking about."

She is so damn rightttt.

"But he would spot us, i dont want that." Riley said, " oh my child,i am a pro just copy me , okay?"

I nodded my head and she crawled on the floor like she was a baby. Some best friend i have .

Well she tried her best and came back with a grin and said ," well for an upgrade they are talking about best friends and Zack is saying how awesome of a friend you are." Riley ended this sentence with a wink and oh my god i was just blushing. I was blushing so bad.

He is talking about me on his date!????? OMGGGGG he is the best he is so perfect. I wish i could hear more , i want to know what he thinks about me.

I couldn't stop myself from staring at Zack. I noticed his smile,the way he combed back his hair, his cheeks were pink because it was cold outside plus he is a but sensitive to this weather, he still looks so adorable. PERFECTION.

It wasn't late till,i noticed Quinn. She was the typical hot babe every guy would fall for. Her makeup was on point and her eyebrows were the definition of FLEEK. Her figure was to die for and wait she didn't have a food baby what the fuck. How is her stomach so flat ?

All the thoughts were hounding me, that's when the thing i feared the most happened.

Quinn came to our table and said," I couldn't help but notice that you were staring at me and my date. What's your problem?" Riley and I were scared as fuck.

This is the end of my life. Why did i have to agree to this? I could have just watched a rom com at home and save my time rather than coming all the way here. Zack will hate me now. My life is such a big mess.

That is when Zack came to my rescue and said," hey Quinn they are my friends calm down, let me handle it you just wait for a bit.

Zack gave me a look and i followed him quietly with my head down ,like i had committed a crime. Zack took my to a corner pulled me and said," what are you doing here? Are you spying on my date? If you had a problem all you had to do is tell! I wouldn't have minded. I just need an answer why are you here?"

Will Zack and Savannah have a fight? Is this how this is going to end? What if Quinn starts dating Zack? Who knows:))

So happy new year to you guys! Sorry this was late but i had to study. Next part will be out soon ;)

Part 6 - What's your type?

He was so close to me,I could feel his breath over mine . I wanted the time to stop that exact minute . I kept staring at his deep blue eyes.

"Anna!!!I want the answer,why are you spying on me and my date?" Zack asked in a demanding voice.I stuttered, and with a bit courage i thought i will let out my feelings but the words that came out were," i heard things about Quinn and wanted to check if she is the right girl u would date or not." Wow way to go! So good at lies huh? Just confess u like him whats the big deal?First lie to your best friend.Woah that haunted me."Since when did u start believing in rumours? U aren't that shallow " said Zack. "Uh.... I mean..... Like ..... You..... Its my fault I am sorry" i said with my head down. Zack lifted my head up,and hugged meWoah he smells so great.I was a bit shocked, the more I wanted to hug him i was still confused . That's when i broke the hug and said ,"are you mad at me?" He laughed and said ,"i could never be mad at you, you are so cute" Awwwww, the more i think the more perfect he becomes.

He continued,"Quinn, is hot for sure but not my type"AAHHHH-HHHAAAAHHHHH,YESYESYES THI IS THE BEST DAY OF MY LIFE OMGOMGOMGOMG.

I calmed myself down and asked,"umm so who is your type?" He thought for a bit and said,"funny,cute, smart ofcourse, understanding and goofy, kind of like you are."

Omgomgomgomgomg!!!!!!!! His type is me? I am his type? Is he saying that we should date like indirectly or something? I mean I would love to ofc.He does seem the same way, doesn't he? I would be totally cool if the world ended right now.

"But i would never date you, you are my buddy" finished Zack .

Well well well, we are back to reality Savannah. There is no chance that a perfect guy like him would date you.Calm your nerves down.ITS NEVER GOING TO HAPPEN.

I fake smiled and said,"Eww, that would so weird, me and you?you and me? Hah never. Right?" "Absolutely,I would never want to destroy the bond be have it's too precious."

Okay i am confused. The guy i like just BESTFRIEND ZONED ME. So i should be sad.But my best friend said our bond was too precious to lose. What is life ?!

"So are we cool?" I asked, he said "ya we are chill, i just gotta go and say bye to Quinn and then i will drop you and riles ." He is such a sweetheart

I texted riley to meet me behind the restaurant,she came really quick and said,"What happened? Is he mad at us? I mean my part doesn't matter. Is he mad at you?" Boy she is a curious one," chill we are cool. He doesn't think that Quinn is her type and plus he is dropping us home." I smiled. "So should I leave you two love birds alone?" Riley smirked and said. "We are not lovebirds, just don't make the car ride awkward,okay?" "Sure,your highness"riley said. We both had a good laugh.

In a while Zack came and said,"let's go,shall we?" He called a cab and he held the gate for me. AwwRiley could not help but smile at us,looks like she is having more fun than me here .

It was awkward as we were all sitting at the back and i was kind of glued to zack, which i liked pretty obvious and riley was trying her best to make us sit closer she took more and more space,she didn't stop until i gave her a sting eye and she apologized with her eyes too giving me that 'okay sorry' look.

Riley got off first as she lived in the second lane. Zack walked me to my house , we talked about how we used to play paintball in his terrace,how he used to dress up as a girl because he really liked white colour i dont even think it's a colour he is weird to be very honest . He may be the jock of the school but he is a softie that too only in front of me, which makes me feel special.

I reached my home and my door was locked. I tried to call my mom and I checked i got a text from her saying-

"Honey, sorry dad and i have to rush to the hospital in the other side of town as their is an emergency surgery case that we have to attend. I talked to mrs.ryder she has arranged a room for you till the time we are out! Love you sweetie take care!"

"Well that's a bummer" i sighed , Zack said ,"you are coming to THE ZACK RYDER'S house, girls die for that apportunity and that's a bummer for you?" Wait omg yeah i have never loved my mom so much before it's perfect! But i have to keep my calm. Chill anna don't panic."Well i am your best friend not the girls with fake eyelashes going 'i love you zack' all the time don't expect that from my bro." BRO?! ARE YOU KIDDING ME?"Yes sure, anna the great i always knew you were a lesbian"Zack said. "Hey? When did i say that?" I asked"I mean look at me anna i am the mr.

Perfect of armadillo high and u have not fallen for me yet that's a shame"
Zack added.

"A shame for you balloon head, i am mighty proud." I said proudly.

"That's what i love about you, you always treat me like a normal friend not
the popular guy, you are the best Anna."

I blushed, i couldn't control my smile obviously. We went to his house and
found a note-

"Zack,we are leaving for your aunt's house as we have to help her with your
cousin's wedding. We know Savannah is coming so the guest room is ready.
We will be back in two days . Make sure you don't get into any trouble"
-love mom and dad.

Well, what a coincidence. Zack and Savannah are left all alone in the night
in Zack's house. What will happen between them? Are things gonna heat
up or nothing would happen?

Haha who knows? Maybe you will when u read the next chapter!! Next
chapter out soon:)

Part 7 - The night at my crush's

I have to spend the night at Zack's!!!!!! Omg how did i get so lucky? I wish cupid hit him with an arrow like he did to me. I mean how can a girl like me be so lucky to spend a night with him? Iknow,iknow we aren't having sex or something but EEEEEEEPPPP!

"Will you walk or should I pick you up ma'am?" Said Zack, bursting my thought bubbles. "I can walk mister! I was just...... Um .... Thinking that i have nothing to wear and i can't sleep in this spy outfit." I said. "Anna you can wear one of my shirts and shots you don't have to think twice about it okay? Now get in i am freezinggg!" Answered Zack.

I get to wear ZACK RYDER'S CLOTHES?! AAAHHHHHHH I mean his shirt would smell like him and i will have is essence while i am sleeping . Awww.

"Get in slowpoke." Shouted Zack. I followed him, i usually never felt weird coming to his house but i am getting this tingling feeling in my tummy which i have never had.Gosh i am too into him.

Zack being a gentleman showed me the guestroom and gave me one of his t - shirts . I obviously couldn't fit into his shorts so i thought being in the black shorts i already had would be more comfortable. While i was going to change Zack stopped me and he had a huge grin on his face, which usually happens when he is upto something mischievous. I got curious ans asked," whatsup? Why are you making such a face?" He said "what if he have a movie night? Like we did during middle school? It used to be so fun! Its been three years since we had one can we have one pleaseee?"

Omg movie night is such a great idea . I used to love our movie nights it was a great experience . I think it would be much better now. Well Anna just be calm and don't get all jumpy while saying yes like you are dying to.

"Answer anna!" He made that cute puppy dog face, which i always hated coz he made me do everything with that one look .

He is so adorable.

"Yeah sure! It would be great till the time i choose what to watch because your taste sucks" i said."In your dreams babe!i have much better taste than you that's why we are gonna watch home alone . Caution- all the parts."

Did he just call me babe?Babeee!!

I got a but nervous and said,"yeah OFCOURSE it's Christmas month home alone to would be great! You are improving BABE." Wow i loved to say that.

"Babe? Seriously what is gotten into you?" Said Zack .

" You are the one who started it, right?"

"Anna's what are you hearing i said BRO, You sure you don't have a hearing problem?"

God! I am hearing stuff . I embarrassed myself pretty well. WAY TO GO SAVANNAH.

"I will go and get changed okay bbye!" I ran off . I went to his room and changed . While i was changing i smelled Zack's shirt and oh my god it was the best feeling ever . I really wanted to know which perfume he used it's very addictive. Its like i am already his girlfriend and he is letting me wear his clothes.

Well i was done chaging so i unlocked the room. Zack didn't change yet so i looked around his room. He had many pictures of him with his parents in vacation,his football team and WAIT! IS THAT ME? OH MY GOSH IT IS ME . HE KEEPS MY PHOTO IN HIS ROOM. Well technically our photo which we took on my birthday, and there was just a photo of me too in which i had cake all over my face. This is the sweetest thing anyone could have ever done for me. Looking that picture now i find it very very cute. Its so considerate that he has my photo in his room. Well for a plus point he has no other girl's picture. Yay!!

"Self obsession much?" A voice said , it was Zack " what are you looking at?"

I said,"i never knew you had my photo in your room, plus u never showed me that you had these. Plus it's very considerate that you have me here.""I have all my special and important moments here."

Awwww he is the best. My birthday is important and special to him? This guy melts my heart in every way possible

Zack continued," i mean it is important as on your birthday the greatest idiot was born."

Well back to square one. Why is he like this. Ughhh

Zack' ms POV - After the party and that kiss dare anna had been acting very different i think this movie night will be a great way to be like we were the way we were . This is a great way to reconnect as it had been weeks since we talked properly and i really love talking to her but after seeing her today in my shirt i couldn't stop but smile at her . My shirt looked like it was made for her not me.I couldn't help but notice how cute she looked in that messy bun, black shorts and my t-shirt. That's what i loved about her, she was completely transparent in front of me, she was herself and never pretended to be someone else and always understood me. And the way she was staring at my picture wall. She could steal anyone's heart. But too bad she is my best friend.____

Oooooooohh !!!!! Does Zack like Savannah too? Does he feel the same way? Will he fall for her or friendzone her?

Hahaha! Who knows?

Read the next chapter to find out:)

(□□□□□)(□□□□□)

Part 8- Movie night

✱ hey guys sorry for updating late I had exams thanks for 300 reads
though:))*

-~-

"This is it, I finally get to have a movie night with Zack! I know it's as best
friends but have you been ever this lucky to have a movie night with your
best fri..... Crush sorry! But it's good we got to bond after so long, YIPEE"
I said to myself.

Zack busted the door open ," I heard someone talking are you talking to
someone? "

"Me? Oh I am not talking to anyone Zack."

"Don't tell me that you have started talking to yourself again! I told you
people would think you are out of your mind, I need you to stop this
Savannah orlove."

"Quit being my mother Zack, I already have one and that's too much."

"Ha I wanted to know how it feels having a child like you."

"In you dreams Ryder , no one is like me, accept me *winks*."

"Yeah ofcourse no one would pull off such a horrible wink."

" You little rat!!!!" I threw a pillow at him but being the jock he is he caught it with one hand showing the intensity of his veins which had me melted. He then threw back it at me much harder than I did . Why do I forget not to throw stuff at him?!!?

"Well if we are done with this pillow fight let's start with our movie night. Please don't sleep again and drool on my shoulder." Said Zack

"What? I don't drool on your shoulder . I am not a baby ."

"You do Anna, you just don't realise it because I am so hot."

Can't deny but he is.

"That makes no sense at all Zack. How is this even related?"

"Many girls fall for that surprisingly you don't . Eh still worth a try."

"Too late for falling for you." I mumbled.

"Are you possessed anna? Stop scaring me let's watch home alone don't delay it and here have the snacks."

He threw some chips packets, popcorns, two cokes and kit Kats.

He really does know me well.

So our movie marathon started. Home alone 1,2,3 . I couldn't help but notice how he laughed, how he smiled he looked adorable.

His chiseled jawline, sharp and highlighted cheekbones and the intensity of his deep blue eyes could kill anyone . No wonder so many girls fell for him.

Zack was right, it was almost 12 at might and being the sleepyhead I am I again slept on his shoulder without realising. His shoulder was very comfortable. I liked being with him even if he thought of us as best friends.

Next day I woke up on Zack's bed. It was 8 in the morning and I couldn't find Zack. I wore the extra slippers he had on his room and went to the kitchen . There were Zack and his parents. Liza and Carol (zack's parents) welcomed me. Both of them were very nice people , infact their love story was very fascinating. Even they started off as best friends.

Liza said," Savannah! So good to see you again! I hope our talk didn't wake you up sweetie."

"Wake her up? Mom she sleeps like she is the sleeping beast." Said Zack. I gave him the angry stare and said," it's sleeping beauty I think you have the wrong movie name."

"For the movie it might be wrong but for you sleeping beast is the best I could come up with. " Said Zack with a little sarcastic laugh.

"Please be quiet you two! Don't act like kids." Mr. Ryder said.

He turned towards me and said," your father called us yesterday, he said both you dad amd mom would be out of town for the next two weeks. They told us where the house key is you should go and get your stuff packed and move here as the thought it would be the best idea. They were a little afraid to let you stay home alone."

"Thanks mr. Ryder . I hope it's no trouble for both of you to let me stay here." I said.

" Oh it's not. Its been long since we talked i would love to have you here you are like our daughter darling, go and get your stuff packed. Its a Sunday so you can go to the bowling alley as Carol's office colleagues are coming. " Said Mrs. Ryder

I beamed a smile at her and went to get my stuff. That's when mom called me told that there was an emergency case at the hospital on the other side of the town and many people were sick so they had to treat them. I totally understood it as their job was difficult and tiring.

Zack's POV-

I knew anna would have slept during the movie marathon because she loves her sleep more than anything in this whole wide world. To let her sleep comfortably I switched off the tv and left the movie in between. I didn't want her sleep to get disturbed.

I noticed her for a bit, how she slept soundly like a baby . Even with messy hair she looked great. I smiled at her. The strand of hair falling on her face was disturbing her so I removed ut and put it behind her ear. I got up and made her lay in my bed and covered her with a blanket. I tidied the room up and patted on her head na d left the room and went to the guest room to sleep.

Pov ends.

I was so excited to go bowling with Zack! It had been so long since we hung out. I wore my white off shoulder and blue jeans and a silver moon necklace. Put on lipgloss and mascara and wore black sneakers. I went to Zack's room to call him he wore back jeans, grey hoodie with denim jacket and white sneakers.

Outfits

We left for the alley and reached there in fifteen. Then I saw the person who I didn't wanna see.

Quinn Forester.____

Sorry guysssss I am late but hope you liked the chapter! I am trying something new by adding the outfits .

If you want a certain person to play as Zack, Savannah,riley or Quinn please suggest!:)

Part 10 - Old friends re-unite

Hey guys I am extremely sorry for such a late update I had exams I promise to make it up to you soon for now here is a chapter:)

Plus I am kinda bummed that my ranking went from 1 to 14 in the popular guy section but 1 in falling for my best friend I don't know whether to happy or sad.

I decided a great plot though during these days. Sorry there would be many cliffhangers (evil laugh)

Just the person I didn't want to see wow . I finally get some time alone with Zack and miss Quinn perfect forester interrupts our dat- um hang out.

Zack went in for a quick hug but Quinn didn't seem to let off him . She held her hand and thought her date went great . Ha sure Quinn you are not even his type okay? I am .

Okay someone like me I got a little on top of my head there.

It wasn't late till I saw a very familiar face there he was bowling and woah he looked like a Greek god. Light brown hair with a proper athlete body, his body looked so toned like he just stays in the gym all day. He has a piercing in his left ear and he looked like all girls would be falling to have a moment with him .

He had such a perfect smile and laugh. His voice was melting me inside the way even Zack's voice never did . Plus his teeth were so white, wait how can you whitewash teeth it's practically impossible.

When I was in my thought world Zack shook my out of it and then Greek god turned out to be quinn's cousin.

Woah hot genes you got in that family.

The Greek god came over and his face lit up when he saw me, he hugged me and said ," oh my god savvy it's been years!"

Okay confusion

But only one person called my 'savvy' and that is oh my god.

"You are Kendall Parker!! My kenny how are you? It's been so long since I met you!" I squealed and went in for a hug.

"What happened to the cute,little goofball I was friend's with? What have you done to that little guy?" I said with a pouty face.

"Hey don't kill me for having a bit of a glow up" ken teased.

Bit of a glow up

Woah I said myself, what a coincidence that both of my crushes are here. I bet I never saw this one coming.

I know I was bummed about Quinn but I didn't third wheel atleast. I had Greek g- ken with me which wasn't awkward at all after all we were summer camp buddies. To be very honest puberty and glow up sure has an accident with Kenny.

I never realised how the time went by because it was two hours since we started bowling. It was one if the best evenings ever. Kendall asked me to get drinks. I was surprised as even after four years he remembered I liked vanilla frappe .

When we were returning Zack and Quinn were no where to be found. Ken and I looked, then we decided to split ways and look for them.

I checked everywhere,but no luck. I was worried about Zack , knowing he wasn't a baby,but still I was worried .

At the end of the alley I found to people taking to each other, though they were standing extremely close. I thought I should not interrupt so I turned my way but then I heard a voice that sounded like Zack saying "You are a really turn me on, let's try that again."

I froze.

I was hoping it was not my zac-

Um just Zack for now. I hope it's not Zack and Quinn.

My palms were sweating. There was a rush of adrenaline in my body as I turned thinking of every possible consequence but I just held on to my trust on Zack when he said Quinn wasn't his type.

I turned and what I saw next, I wasn't ready for it.

It was Zack, but the girl wasn't Quinn I tried to figure out who she was as my tears blurred my eyes.

No.

This can't be true.

It can't be her! For his sakes!!

But it was true. The bitch, crazy attention seeking ex girlfriend Brittany Adams and Zack Ryder were having a full makeout session.

How could he?

He was so into hating her, she cheated on him and still he chose that bitch?!

After all this I ran away from the place with tears rolling down my cheeks. Even if I tried to stop it was involuntary, I was heart broken.

I knew I never had a chance with Zack but I never thought he would go back to that attention seeking slut!

I was so in pain I didn't notice that there was a hand on my shoulder.

I hoped it would Zack saying that he was drugged and that's why he kissed Brittany and came here to apologise to me but to my surprise it was Kendall.

He sat down beside me and said, "how long?"

I looked up and asked,"what?"

He then said ,"how long have you had a crush on Zack?"

"I don't know , I always liked him I guess it was just too late till I realised that I genuinely had a big crush on him. I forgot that I am just his best friend I can never be his girlfriend or anything, I should have stayed in my lane, I know getting into anything with him will just hurt me."

Even though I was crying I could see how Kendall's expressions dropped at an instant.

I pulled me closer and said ,"savvy , you are one of the most beautiful and amazing people I have known okay? Don't cry and hurt me like that."

He leaned closer and gave me a tight hug, caressing my back. In some time I felt better I looked at him and gave a weak smile.

He held my hand and said ," I know this is not the best timing to ask you this but I think it will help you heal the pain."

I had a bit hope and asked,"what?"

He said looking into my eyes

"You should date me Savannah."

Haha guys I am back!!

What do you think of this chapter?

Do you ship Kenny and savvy? How do you like their chemistry?

What do you think if Zack now? Still rooting for #zacannah?

What do you think will Savannah say after this bomb that Kendall threw?

Share your views , comments on this chapter.

Vote and share too!!

Until next time lovess

Part 11 - New relationships

K endall's Pov

Flashback

Savannah Orlove, my savvy , the girl with two pigtails and cherry sweet scent.

I first met her in summer camp in Georgia. That time I used to be the fat kid who was bullied by everyone. I always used to cry during the nights due to the teasing and ate chocolate to reduce my pain (haha classic) .

I was tired by the bullying , but one day a girl with two pigtails, a light blue shirt with a denim jumpsuit came over to the place where everyone used to tease and bully me.

She immediately held my hand and stood in front of me and said ," Hey you losers! If you don't get away from him this right second I will complaint your parents and camp instructor!! Don't you dare try to tease him again or else you will have it from me do you get that?"

That second I smiled well I blushed because nobody ever did that for me. I liked her since then (as a friend) .

During the camp we got closer and spent more time together, I started calling her savvy and she called me kenny, no one teased me and I hated when someone else tried to be friends with savvy instead of me.

After that every year I wanted to go for camp. I begged my parents to let me go because I never wanted to missa chance to be with savvy.

But as I became a teenager I realised all these years me being protective and possessive about her wasn't as a friend. I liked her, I REALLY liked her.

It was a bummer when I got to know when you are thirteen you can't attend the camp as it is for kids only. When I got to know this I cried so bad that I got a fever next day. A week later my parents decided to meet the Orlove 's I was so excited I took a two hour bath, brushed my hair a hundred times, put up cologne and waited for savvy to come.

We had the best time and when she was going she turned to me and noticed that I was almost in tears she gave me a hug. I held her so tightly that she stopped breathing for a second I guess, but it felt like she perfectly fit into my arms and I perfectly fit into hers.

She broke the hug and said ," you will always be my best friend kenny no matter what. I love you and I will miss you. "

I was so overwhelmed by hearing the words 'i love you' from her mouth that I gave her quick peck on her cheek and then she left, I could see her blush, oh lord she looked cute . My first crush,my first attachment and my best friend left.

Over all these years I thought I would forget about her. I even dated two girls but never for a long term I only had savvy on my mind , how she must be doing right now,how much she would have changed and the most important thing 'did she remember me?'

During sophomore year I found a guy in my school, Brian Adams turns out he was friends with Savannah and dated her best friend for a year I think because all I cared during that conversation was savvy,my savvy.

Then he showed me her one of her Instagram posts, oh boy was I stunned. She grew up to be so beautiful, so pretty her honey brown eyes, her brown hair, lightly tanned skin and her precious smile. She was flawless .

In the mid of the hallway I was smiling like crazy. I stalked her Instagram for two whole hours.

I couldn't help but notice a guy who she had in her stories and some posts too. Oh boy I was jealous, my arms turned into a fist and my jaw clenched when I saw her hanging out with another guy it was some guy named Zack spider or Ryder something. I prefer to call him spider.

But Brian reassured me that they were best friends and nothing else so I calmed down a bit or else the spider must have been dead by now.

Present

Seeing how savvy cried when she saw Zack kiss some girl broke my heart not only the fact that she was crying, but the thought that I lost my savvy. I wanted her all these years and she is mine some spider can't come and steal savvy from me not even Savannah had this right.

So the moment I had been waiting since the past 5 years came.

I asked her out .

I could see her confusion when I asked her to date me I know this was a bit sudden for her but I wanted to make my five years of wait worth it.

Pov ends

"What?" I asked I never thought Kendall would ask me out he was my first crush,my first attachment and my best friend but I never thought your crush likes you back. I mean after all these years when I like someone else he asks me out.

I am on the verge of my heartbreak and he has the audacity to ask me out? What part of a best friend does he not get?

What if he is really Into me and me and Zack were never really meant to be and kenny was the one?

All these thoughts were running when he continued and said

"Savvy I know you are heartbroken and I know you like him but I was talking about what if we fake date and make him jealous? And he realises his mistake and comes to you? After all a man always wants what he doesn't have right?"

Yes fake date . Why would a Greek god, heavenly looking guy date me? He would have many girls after wanting to be his.

"I know this is pretty fast but take your time and decide but not too much okay? I have too many girls waiting for me ."

"Hey shut up!" I giggled and punched him.

"Ow savvy you killed me?" He said laughing.

Kendall's pov

Ha little did she know fake dating her would be the best time of my life. All these years I wanted to be with her and now I finally have the chance.

Plus how dumb I am to say that I have many girls waiting?! Stupid ugh I just wish she doesn't start hating me.

That's when Zack came out holding Brittany's hand and he stopped for a bit. He looked drunk , I knew savvy was uncomfortable so I held her hand and caressed my thumb over it.

Zack said,"hey Anna guess what I got back with britanny we are sorted out."

Savannah tightened her grip on my hand and said something that shook me.

"That's good for you Ryder even I am dating Kendall now."

She turned towards me and kissed me. I was shocked I didn't how and what to react.

But this was my first kiss with the girl I always dreamt of having it with . I held her waist tightly pulling her closer and deepening the kiss. Gosh her lip balm was sweet .

She broke the kiss and smiled. That smile melted my heart and I hugged her.

After all this time my wish came true.

Savvy was mine now, spider bro gotta step back your Kendaddy is here.

Aaaahhh I fkn love this chapter!! What about you guys?

How did u like Kendall's and Savannah' s back story?

What about Zack huh?

Bbye for now tho gotta go sleep

Part 12 - Fake boyfriends and exes

D id I just did what I did?

I kisses kenny? My best friend ken,kenedy?!

I freaking kissed Kendall Parker?!

What in the world was I trying to do? I destroyed my friendship with him we will never be the same again. One wrong move and I lost my best friend! I am such a doofus!

I did all this just to make Zack jealous? I kissed someone...... Okay I kissed my best friend to make my crush aka now EX best friend jealous? Who does not even like me the way I do? How big of a dumbhead am I?

I couldn't help but these thoughts kept hovering my mind as I thought kissing kenny was the biggest mistake ever . I think I pushed the fake dating thing a bit too much because seeing Zack and Brittany back together made a bunch of emotions flow inside me.

Trust breaker Zack.

Betrayal.

Liar.

Cheat.

Fucking asshole.

And why did kenny kiss me back such passionately?

The last time we talked he said he hated Brittany so much that if she was the last girl on this whole planer he would rather decided to be gay and he wanted full on revenge.

This is how he wanted the revenge? By doing the same thing over again? And hurting me so bad that my heart was crushed into so many pieces that I went off limits and kissed Kenn? Does that Zack butthead Ryder care about my feelings or not?!

I was so mad that I made a pact to myself that not to ever talk again to Zack as he did make a big mistake and he didn't deserve me as a friend no matter how it hurted me.

I couldn't help but notice two things that Zack was tumbling while walking and Brittany tried the best to keep him straight,it was like he had been drugged or something.

But he wasn't looking this drugged when he was sucking Brittany's face out.

Shut up brain.

What a mean person you are, anna.

I still couldn't get why would kenny kiss me back at such an impulse, it was like he was waiting for this moment that he grabbed the opportunity when he got it.

Not gonna lie but he was good.

You are not much help stupid brain!

Hey calm down I am your sub consciousness I am just overthinking it's kind of my job ?

Yea right you are the reason half of my life is fucked up, stop doing what you do!

No can do sorry!

While I was on a imaginary fight with my 'sub consciousness' I forgot how dumb I was looking . It was not too late till I saw kenny staring at me and said,

"Hey I know I am not that good of a kisser ,I mean I think but don't give me that disgusted look it was my first time!"

I continued, "first of all I was talking to myself and second that your are actually pretty grea--"

I noticed how Ken's lips cracked into a bit of a smirk.

What the hell were you going to say savvy mcstupid?!

"I mean let's just forget about it."

Kendall said,"you can't expect me to forget my first kiss. Not fair!"

"Wait! A guy like you hasn't had his first kiss?"

"What do you mean a guy like me?"he said.

"I mean you are so attractive not to forget undeniably hot and that voice can melt my heart plus the perfume you are wearing is already sending me Shivers." I said to myself.

"You find me attractive?" Kendall side with a bit of hope and smile on his face.

I got awkward and as I was Answer him I got a call on my phone it was from riley.

"Hey where the hell are you? Do you know how much crisis am I in? You gotta reach here ASAP or I may die."

Woah even riley is in a mood.

"Yes I am coming riles calm down okay? I will be there in fifteen."

And she cut the call, I wondered what could be so important that even riley is panicking.

I turned to Kendall and asked if he could drop me to riley's . He readily accepted and led me to his car.

I turned around to see Zack but he already left.

Now I know what a heart break feels like.

While we were in the car I asked kenny to play some songs and I asked not to play sad songs . So he played 'Bohemian Rhapsody by queen.'

That song instantly made me smile and I saw that kenny also smiled as he saw me smile . I continued and said,"it mine and Zack's fav--'"

I stopped remembering what all happened in the alley. Tears began falling down and I saw Kenny's hand's grip getting tighter on the steering wheel.

I wiped my tears and said," it's better to forget about what happened, what he did was wrong." And gave a weak smile.

Soon I reached to riley' s house , as I was walking kenny pulled me closer, hugged me and said,

"Thank you for today savvy, you made my first kiss worth it and the fake boy friend deal? It is still on, I will be waiting for you."

I broke the hug, my cheeks were warm and the way kenny's hug made me feel I never felt that way I blushed and gave him a quick peck on his cheek.

I turned and started walking . I dkmt know what stopped me I turned around and said,

"Hey Kendall! "

"What?" He shouted back.

"Will you be my fake boyfriend?" I said.

"I am yours Savannah Orlove" He smiled and got into his car.

Oh my god i was blushing too much as I rang riley's doorbell.

As riley opened the gate , I could see she wasn't in a good condition, it looked like she had been crying and wrapped my arms around her and asked," riley what happened?"

"He is back anna."

"Who? " I questioned.

"Brian, Brian Adams."

Hey peeps! I know this chapter isn't that long but it's all I got for now. So to make it up for you the next chapter coming out on 18 will have many twists and turns and ofc drama.

I just have one exam left . Woohoooo!

So how do you think will the 'fake boyfriend deal' turn out?

Do you ship #sanny? (Better than sandal ,lol)

And do you remember Brian? Don't tell me you don't you have to:(

If you do, I love you

Plus take care and share your views!!

Part 13 - Rebounds

I was there, it broke my heart to see riley like this I know what she went through when Brian Adams , that two timing dog who cheated on my best friend on her birthday.

Flashback to Riley's sixteenth birthday

"Happy Birthday!!"

The whole room shouted, I had never seen riley so happy. According to riley her life was going perfect right now all her family problems were sorted , she had a great relationship going on with Brian,her grades were impressive and she didn't have anything to worry about.

I was so happy because my best friend was happy she had been with me through every problem and I did the same and seeing her genuinely happy was great.

All the people from school came, everyone was partying hard and dancing
.

Well other than her birthday it was riley and Brian's 18 month anniversary, yeah I know it's a good amount of time. Everyone wanted to have a relationship like them, it showed how much they loved each other. Even after

18 months they stayed the same and didn't let anything get between them. Well at that time riley, Brittany and I were best friends, later we got to know Brittany used us, specifically me to get close me to Zack, which I never had a problem with before, but now I realise how stupid I was to do that.

As we were dancing riley bumped into someone and got something on her dress. It was guacamole though it didn't stain much it was still noticable.

She tugged me and said that I should help her choose another dress. I tagged along with her but as we opened the door, we saw something we should not have seen.

A girl from riley's neighborhood, Tina I think was all over Brian.

They were sucking each other's faces and acted like everything was normal.

"What the fuck is going on here?!" Riley shouted even though I could see her eyes tearing up.

Before Brian could speak riley took him by his collar and slapped him.

"How could you do this to me? Was I not enough?! After all this time u cheated in me with my neighbour? And that too on my birthday? Do you have a heart or there is just a stone in its place? I loved you Brian Adams! You broke me!" Riley screamed.

She stormed out of the room , before follow her I gave Brian and death glare and said,"get the hell out of here you don't deserve someone like her."

Brian said," Savannah try to understand I don't know what happened I thought it's riley I swear to god I really love her I dotmt know what to do without her please help me!"

"Helo the person who cheated on my best and claims to be in love with her? Oh piss off asshole." I said and went to find riley.

Flashback ends

"How did you know he is back?" I asked.

Riley showed me her chat.

Unknown number

Hey how are you?

I am sorry who is this?

You know me, I am back for you Ri. I want you back I love you.

—————————————————————————————

Everyone knew only Brian called riley 'Ri'. If anyone else excluding me called her he/ she was dead, he was really possessive of her.

"I don't know what to do, why is he back? He can't hurt me every damn time. I went for a therapy because of him I almost failed all my classes and he says 'i love you' does he know what these words mean?" Riley said.

I know how heartbroken she was at that time.

"No I can't do this, I am not going to cry over him now . He has hurt me a lot. I know what I will do now." Riley said.

Me being my curious self asked,"what are you going to do then?"

"It's time for a rebound anna, like u have Kendall hottie Parker, I will go for Spencer holder."

Wait wait, how did she know about Kenny, and she is going after Spencer? The guy who had been crushing on her since kindergarten? Woah what has happened to my best friend.

Spencer holder:)

"Uhh how did you know about kenn-- I mean Kendall?" I asked.

Wiping her tears she came back to her sassy face and said,"I may have been crying but I do have eyes to see what my best friend is up to, for an update yes I approve him for you because he clearly likes you."

I could not unhear that statement

'he clearly likes you'

'he clearly LIKES YOU'

Does he really like me? Like um like like me? Is that true? Is that why he wanted to date me? But I think I like him too I mean I lov-- like Zack hut after what he did Today I can't even look at him the same.

"Earth to anna?" Riley said.

"I have to tell you something riles."

That's when I said everything about Zack and Brittany, my fake dating deal and how the night turned out.

Riley's face was priceless, she had her eyes glued on me and barely managed to speak, before she could say anything someone rang the doorbell.

We went down and opened the door. There was a guy who has some cuts on his face and was limping before he could lift his head it up.

Zack.

Hello babies!! Ew no

Hello guys!!(much better)

I know this is not much of a chapter , but I wanted to write one though I was having a headache.

What do you think happened to zack? Why is he covered with bruises and how'd you like the new addition? Spencer?

Do comment your views , vote and share the story:)

Part 14 - Zack's regret

There he was, take the support of the door, barely able to stand. Wounds on his face, had a cut on his hand. It looked like someone had brutally hit him, even though I had this thought of me hating Zack after this eventful night, seeing him in such a condition hurt me more than anything.

Before he could speak, I took his hand in mine, kept his other hand on my shoulder and held him by his well built waist. Riley was also in shock though she helped me to carry Zack.

Even for the both of us he was very heavy, we carefully made him sit on a couch, in such a position that he was comfortable.

I couldn't see Zack in such a condition , I could see the way he was looking at me, I could sense that he was apologizing. Even though he was weak I could still understand his expressions.

He was about to say something but I cut him off and said,

"Where the fuck have you been Ryder? And what has happened to you? It's like you were about to get killed! You were with Brittany right? What someone tried to flirt with your hot ex-- sorry no you 'girlfriend' so you beat them up? But they turned out to be stronger than you so you got beat up? And what she broke up with you again that's why you are here?!"

Hey calm down go easy on him my subconscious said to me.

"Calm down anna he is hurt, wait I will get the first aid box." Riley said and went off to bring the first aid box

"I am sorry anna, I don't why are you so upset and full of anger I can explain." Zack said.

"Explain? What will you explain? You can barely drink water in this condition I don't think you can explain." I rudely replied.

I know I am going very hard in him but what he did was just not acceptable. He hurt me, he hurt me very bad and he deserved what he is going through right now.

Before I could get up and leave he held my hand and pulled me back, even after getting so badly hurt god knows how he is still able to pull a person back.

" I was drugged, I met Brittany at the alley and she begged me to take her back when I said no she insisted but when I was about to leave she asked me if she could buy me a drink for old times sake ans said this would be the last time she ever crossed ways with me, I agreed but everything that happened after that was a blur. I remember waking up in a garage and hearing Brittany say ," beat him up till he is begging me to take him back and that he accepts that he loves me" I got up with the energy I had left and tried to find they guys but I couldn't, I was too weak. I somehow managed to come here because I knew you would not have gone home alone so you must have come to Riley's."

My heart skipped a beat when I heard what Zack had to say, I turned around gave him an apologetic look and hugged him.

"I am sorry I kept thinking the worst case scenarios after I saw you and Brittany together I kind of lost it and I was very mad at you. I am sorry." I apologised Zack.

"Seriously a second ago I could have sworn u wanted to rip his head of ." A voice said from behind, it was riley.

Zack and I had a small laugh. Riley and I bandaged him up and gave him a paracetamol to reduce the pain. He managed to get to the guest room. Riley got a call from her parents whi were out of town for a wedding, si she went to attend the call. I tucked Zack in the bed . As I was about to leave he asked

"Why did you kiss Kendall Parker?"

Zack's Pov

Even though some things were blur I still couldn't take the image out of my head of Savannah kissing Kendall. I don't know why it bothered me, I couldn't help myself from asking her this question.

I knew Savannah won't kiss Kendall without a reason, Because she wasn't a girl like that I knew her really well

When I asked the question I could see her face turn blank.

First I just wanted to know why she did so, now it bothered me, it was a really weird feeling which I wasn't able to understand. If it were any other guy I maybe would not have reacted this much, but anna used to really like that Kendall.

Plus what kind of a name is Kendall? Isn't it a girl's name like that Kendall Jenner?

I instantly hated that name now, I don't know why but I did.

Pov ends

" You must have been dreaming Zack, I didn't kiss Kenny." I said

"Oh kenny? You have got nicknames for each other? Since when may I ask?" Zack asked.

" Since when have you been so nosy? Plus you should be happy I got me first boyfriend." I gave a smirk and said.

" Excuse the fuck me? What the hell,? It can't be true you met like three hours ago and you are already dating?" Zack blurted out

Did I really just say that? Why am I trying so hard to make him jealousy?? Ughh

"I mean we clicked really well Today and I got to know even he liked me during the summer camp I wish he did so he asked me out on a date next weekend." I blushed

" You know what I am going to sleep." Zack said . Boy he seemed pissed .

I chuckled and left the room. I was walking down the stairs as a voice stopped me " if I were you I would know that Zack is a bit jealous."

Riley.

" You need to stop sneaking up like that riles." I said.

" And you need to stop acting like you are dumb, get the hint he likes you he just doesn't get that yet."

"Well when he gets that then we'll see okay? Good night Sherlock."

I bid goodbye and went to sleep. Before going to bed I checked my phone and I saw a text from an unknown number .

"Goodnight princess <3"

I was confused so I replied.

"Who is this?"

"Kenny here princess<3"

"Oh hey, plus it's late kenny go to sleep :)"

"I will when you do babygirl"

" I am feeling special, I didn't know you had a romantic bone in your body"

"For you, yes princess <3"

Woah I blush bad, princess and babygirl? What is up with my Kenny?

____

Helloooooo!! How did you like this chapter??

Turns out Zack isn't the bad guy here. Hmm

And ooh princess? Haha cute right? I wish someone called me that too:(

And keep on reading and voting,you guys inspire me to write more<3

Love love

Part 15 - First date

Hey guys sorry for the delay! I have been utilising my time in doing dance routines, workout,chores, catching a rat and studying. Yes I started for eleventh already, no I am not a nerd I studied for 30 mins.

Plus I am a very boring person, I don't watch shows or movies . You guys have no idea how this lockdown is going for me.

***

The night was over pretty quick, though I woke up late. I went to riley's dining room and say riley and her mom chatting. Riley's mom hugged me and said ," look how much have you grown darling, you are getting prettier by the day." I gave her a smile and thanked her.

"So kiddies I gotta go to work, I made pancakes and maple syrup for the breakfast helo yourself okay? And make sure Zack took his medicines he got pretty hurt. I still can't believe he fell of a tree while saving a cat. Anyway, I gotta go. Have fun!" Mrs. Pemberton said.

"For a smart businesswoman she is pretty dumb for believing that Zack tried to save a cat." Riley laughed and said.

That's when I got a call from my mother .

" Hey sweetie how are you?"

"I am fine mom. How are the patients?"

"They seem to be getting worse, some of them were fully cured but due to the fire some were badly injured and still are under observation."

"That's sad. When are you guys returning."

"Oh babygirl, it breaks my heart but it may take another weak for us to comeback. I talked to Mrs. Ryder you can stay there, she is very welcoming."

"Okay mom take care of yourself . I miss you."

"We miss you more anna, we will be back soon"

And I cut the call. It never bothered me that my parents weren't home most of the times. I understood their work, one day even I want to be a doctor, an oncologist to be specific. I lost my aunt when I was 8, she died due to pancreatic cancer, it really upset me because she was always there for me when my parents were out. I was really close to her and I still miss her.

As we were getting breakfast, Zack came and stretched himself flaunting his muscular bady with perfect abs. Woah adrenaline rush.

"Good morning riley and the 'girl who didn't tell me she was dating someone'." said Zack.

Me? Dating ? Who? Oh shit I am dating zac- Kendall.

Fake dating to be precise.

"Why are you getting jealous bro?" Snapped riley

"I am not jealous,I think being her best friend I have the right to know stuff, specially when it comes to other guys." Replied zack

"Knock it off you two, I am hungry Lemme eat." I replied stuffing my mouth with pancake.

" Messy as always." Said Zack with a cute smile and wiped off the maple syrup off my lips with his thumb and licked at " hmm your mom is a great cook riley."

I was in shock.

Did he just? Oh my god.

What is this boy doing to me

I looked at riley who almost shit out juice out of her mouth when she saw Zack doing so.

She tugged my top and whispered, "get a hint you dingus! He likes you."

"Oh shut up." I replied.

We heard a knock on the door and Zack opened it .

" I am here for savvy." A familiar voice said.

"Sorry no savvy lives here lover boy, buhbye!!" Said Zack .

Riley and I went to the door, kenny was standing there with flowers.

Wait with flowers?!

Is he going to propose me?

No.

Yes ?

Maybe?

He looks adorable.

Wait?

Oh my God.

"What are you doing here kenny?"I asked him

"I wanted to ask if you wanted to go on a date? In the restaurant down-town?" He asked.

How could I say no to this face?

But why is he taking me out on a date? Aren't we fake dating?

"Umm....I ..... Yes sure! I would love to! I will be ready at 7." I replied.

His face lit up like a bulb. "I will be there princess."

He have me the flowers and left.

"That's great anna!" Riley exclaimed and hugged me. "Even I had to go on a date with Spencer how about a double date?"

"Shit no! It will be your first date . We won't disturb. We will get another table which is a bit far away. Okay?" Riley said

"Sure riles it's perfect!" I said.

"You are really gonna go? With that male barbie doll?" Asked Zack with a concerned look on his face.

"Should I not?" I asked hopefully expecting a reply like

"Please don't go be with me."

But reality is hurtful, he said "ofcourse go I will go home and do something more interesting." He turned and left .

" Well that's rude." I said to myself

***

The day passed quickly and it was time for me and riley to get ready for our date. Zack had left after lunch.i was a nervous wreck as it was my first date . Firsts are always special so it's normal to be nervous.Like Zack' s and mine kiss, it was my first kiss and still was very special.

As I am not amazing with my clothes and riley being a total fashion Diva helped me with the clothes. To be honest , the dress she picked up were breathtaking.

My look-

Riley's look -

Even our dates shock us.

Kendall's look-

Spencer's look -

Exactly at 7 kenny and Spencer reached.

"Why did you ask me out? You said we weren't actually dating." I curiosly asked.

" We have to make it beleivable right?" Kendall answer

"And yeah, princess you look more beautiful today." He complimented

I blushed I blushed so bad Maybe because no one complimented like that before or it was shocking and very sweet coming from kenny.

We reached the restaurant in 10 minutes,it wasn't an awkward ride. Riley decided to come in the other uber with Spencer as she didn't want to 'interfere'.

***

Zack's Pov -

They just met like last night and there already going k dates and kissing each other? That's too fast If you ask me. I know he is Anna's first crush but that's doesn't matter I am her best friend she should atleast talk to me about it .

I don't why I was acting this way because I never acted like this for anyone. I have always been protective of Anna because I don't want her to get hurt, because if someone hurts her it hurts me more. She had been with me through thick and thin . I am very attached to her.

I never felt this weird if she hung out with a guy before mostly because she never liked those guys , but, now that she is out with a guy it really bugs me.

Why am I feeling stuff like this?

____

Hey guys! How'd you like the chapter?

Do you think Zack lies anna? Or he is just a very good best friend?

Hmmm

Who knows?

Hah I do:)

Btw we are very close to 1k reads! I know it's not much but it makes me happy and proud:)

See ya soon

16 - History repeats

Sorry guys I am more than a well late for this chapter! But I have been a busy and lazy and obsessing over TVD.

Damon Salvatore -

***

Zack's Pov -

I went back home, all I could think was of Anna's date with that golden boy even tho he wasn't a blond. I reached home,thumped to my bed and just lay there watching the ceiling.

In a bit I got a text from a friend of mine Greg, "Bro, did sav have a glow up or what? Look at her snap stories."

I got curious and checked and oh biy was I stunned.

□

She looked like an angel from heaven. She looked so perfect even it was a blurred picture. I just wish I was the one who asked her out then it hit me.

She is your best friend dick head! Snap out of it

I lifted myself up and saw my picture wall, there were some pics of me and anna which weren't good because I used to have craves and specs at that time . The look that I hated, but at that time when other girls used to stay away from me anna never left my side.

I even had some solo pictures of Anna which made me smile a bit

Not gonna lie she had an amazing glow up.

I don't why but I really wanted to see her now but she was on a date with that Goldie . So it would be wrong.

Wait! When I was in a date with Quinn she came too just to check if she was the 'right one' . Well it's my time to be the good best friend now.

Pov ends.

Going out with Kenny didn't seem so bad . Even though I liked Zack but I felt really happy with Kenny . I don't know why but everytime I look into his warm brown eyes I have butterflies .

Ew when did I be such a girl?

I could see that even riley was very happy with Spencer, not gonna lie they make a very cute couple . I was happy for her, finally moving on from that nightmare Brian.

"So a white pasta with olives, chicken and oregano for the lady and a double cheese chicken pizza for me." Kendall ordered.

"How do you know that?" I asked

"Um it's pretty simple actually , you call the waiter and tell him what you wanna eat." He replied.

"I meant what I like to eat, how do you know that? Wait have you been stalking your fake girlfriend?" I replied with a sinisterly look.

"No I just remember you mentioning it okay? I don't stalk my fake girlfriends." He replied shyly.

" GirlfriendS you say? Hmmm how many have you had before?" I asked

"I am very glad to mention it, that you are my first savvy." He replied with a very genuine smile.

I had never seen him smile like that before with anyone else. Yes I am guilty, but what can I do? I am a virgo I notice things like these okay? Don't kill me for that.

The date was going great, even though it was a fake date but it didn't feel like one.

As I was eating I remember how Zack and I used to fight over the pasta my mum made when we were little. At the end it used to be us getting grounded, two kids who had white sause pasta all over them and broken plates.

As I was thinking this I looked up and saw Zack.

What the hell is he doing here?!

Is he taking revenge on me for barging Into his date with Quinn?

Oh my god i am so not ready for this right now.

***

Hey I know it's a short chapter but you know writer's block. It sucks. I am currently out of ideas but the new chapter will be out be tomorrow or the next day. I gotta work on some ideas.

Bye and sowyy:(

17 - Date crash

- -

Kendall's POV

Okay what the hell is he doing here? It's mine and savvy's date he cant just come here like she is his.

He has already made her cry enough, I can't let that happen again. Even though I know she doesn't like me like I do but I can never let her get hurt specially not by this spider.

I could see savvy's attention move from me to him. The one day I get to spend with her this knuckle head comes to destroy it. It won't happen now, atleast not when I am on a date with her.

Pov ends

"Hey, can I talk to you?" Zack said.

At this point I was very confused . Why is he even here? I was having a pretty good time with Kendall and being with Kenny made me forget about Zack drama too.

As I was about to speak kenny interrupted and said "she won't talk Zack, we are on a 'date' and you have actually you are interrupting it, after an hour or so you can talk to her so for now please go."

Boy someone's a bit jealouuss my head said.

He I jealous I guess he isn't. Why would he be?

Who knows maybe he likes you.

Kenny? Likes me? Ha no he can get whoever he wants and I am not the one

Keep telling yourself that honey.

"It's really important sav,umm it's.... About your mom and dad." He stuttered.

"What? What happened are they okay? They didn't tell anything." I was worried as hell .

"Just come with me and we will talk about it okay? You can continue your date some other time. I am sorry." Said Zack.

I apologised to Ken, gave him a peck on his cheeks and went with Zack.

Gosh Kendall smells delicious.

Ugh stop it.

"What happened to mum and dad will you please tell it's been ten minutes since we have been walking, please tell I am worried." I said Zack

He looked in my eyes and said, "sav ..... Um I don't know if you would like it or not."

"Give it up already Zack! Please tell me they are my parents!" I almost shouted .

Before he could continue, I got w call from riley

"Please come back here, he ..... He is here . I don't know what to do Anna please come." She said between her tears.

"What happened riley? Don't cry please tell me clearly." I asked her.

"Brian is back, he saw me on a date with Spencer and now he is beatimg the hell Outta him." She said.

"Oh my god , wait there I am coming." I said to her and cut the call.

"What is it? You seed tensed?" Zack asked .

"You didn't tell me about my parents you don't get to know about this okay? Just come with me Ryder." I snapped at him.

We bith ran back to the restaurant and saw a big crowd over there. Zack and pushed people and went inside the crowd.

"How the hell did you ask her out? You dared to ask riley out on a date when you knew I love her? I left town and you turn into a back stabber? Yoy asshole!!" Brian shouted and hit Spencer.

Not gonna lie but Brian Adams had a glow up in these years huh?

It is not the time right now for it!

Sometimes subconscious can be a bitch.

Hey I get hear that!

Zack did his best and with some other guys the fight finally stopped. Brian tried ti talk to riley but she shoved him off and went home. I wanted to go with her but she wanted to stay alone.

Zack got injured too so I took him to my house. The whole ride we didn't talk. I wanted to ask but he was hurt so I thought maybe it wasn't the best timing.

We reached home I dressed up his wounds it stung a bit. It must have I was applying a bit extra pressure on the wounds because I was mad at him . If he wouldn't have taken me from there I would have been there for riley . I can't even imagine what she is going through right now.

"Will you tell me or not?" I asked.

"What should I tell you sav?" Zack answered.

"Oh don't you sav me, tell me why did you get me out of my date?" I again questioned.

"You did the same didnt you?" He shot back

"I never pulled you out Ryder, you ce after me. Plus I didn't lie about your family like you did ."

I could see that he was guilty . He knew what he did was wrong. But why would he do something like this in the first place?

He is jealous

Seriously first kenny and then Zack . You should stop it right now ms subconscious.

One day I will be right and then you we will see

"I believe you owe me an explanation Zack. I am waiting."

He looked up to me . Came closer, kept on coming closer. Looked into my eyes and

Then he kissed me.

18 - Something has changed

I stood there like a rock. I didn't know how to react or what has just happened. All I know is that I was there, he was there with his hands on my face. I could see the intensity of his blue eyes. We both could sense that there was some tension between us at that moment.

Being his best friend I should have pushed him away, but something inside me stopped me. We bith were speechless. Zack Ryder has actually kissed me. For what reason no one knows.

"What did you just do Zack?"

I was waiting for him to speak up . It's like he was about to say something but he couldn't he was there, standing still. He never acted this strange, it's like I saw a different version of him. He knew that I was dating Kendall even though it wasn't real but fir the people it was and Zack may be the popular guy and all but he would never try and get with a girl who is dating someone else.

"I don't know what did I just do Savannah, I .... Will just leave. It's not right for me to stay here. I will talk to you later maybe." He barely could speak.

Before I could stop him he Stormed of the door and left me all alone in my house. I could not figure out what was going on with him or me at this moment.

I wanted to talk to someone but riley had her own problems to deal with, Zack wasn't picking up my calls .

So the only person I am left with is Kendall.so I dialed his number.

Kendall's Pov

For what that spider did to my date today. It was my first date with savvy and he ruined it. I couldn't hate this guy more at this point.

But I loved the time I had spent with savvy. It may have been short but it was worth it. The way she laughed it my dumb jokes and her smile , I was simply smitten by it.

While I was going through the snaps we clicked , savvy called me.

What can I say? Speak of the angel.

"Hey I need to talk to you kenny."

"Ya sure whatsup?"

"Something happened. I am afraid you might not like it."

"Hey hey calm down. Tell me what happened?"

"Umm remember when Zack said there was a family emergency so I had to leave the date?"

"Yea." How can u forget that spider ruined my date .

"Actually there was no emergency. So we came back and he kind of......"

"He what? What did he do?"

"He kissed me."

This sentence was enough to rise my temper. As if I already didn't despise him enough.

"Did you kiss him back?"

"Yes."

And this sentence was enough to break my heart into a thousand pieces. I never thought this would happen. Its like a part of me broke inside.

"Hey Ken are u listening I have ranted for more than like a minute now, are you okay?"

I couldn't let her know how I was really feeling at that moment. She thought the dating and all was fake but it was the most real thing I have had. It's not her fault though I am the one who made her think it was fake.

"Yea yes, I am good and woah he kissed you. Didn't expect that."

"That's all you have to say?"

"What else can I say? He maybe likes you . Mission accomplished I guess."

"Okay that's weird Ken . I am gonna go to bed ."

"Hey listen savvy, let's breakup this fake relationship now that you have zack."

"You sure?"

"Yes we are still best friends though."

I cut the call and went to my terrace which was my happy,sad, thought processing phase. I just sat there looked above in the sky. I couldn't manage to hold back the tears I had in my eyes.

Pov ends

I was kind of bothered by Ken's reaction. Even though I know we fake dated but I grew attatched to him not in the best friend way. I felt really good when I was with him and it never looked fake. It always seemed very real.

Why the hell do I have so many complications at once? God kill me please.

I was about to sleep when my parents called to check in on me. They said they would be back by next week and there is a surprise for me. Well I am not really a big fan of surprises at this current moment. But atleast my parents would be home soon, so much has happened since they left for their medical camp.

I went to the kitchen to get some ice cream and French fries. Yes it may sound disgusting but it tastes good. Food as always been my escape from my problems.

I have a certain motto to deal with all my problems since I was a kid.

Stress? Food.

Exam tension? Food.

Cramps? Food.

Existential crisis? Food.

Non existent relationship problems? FOOD.

I bet this is the motto of every teenager.

My mom called again after an hour or so when I had drowned my self in food and binge watching the vampire diaries.

"Hey honey I got to her that Kendall's family is back in town. So we are going out for camping next weekend with Zack's family."

" You mean us with the Parker's and Ryder's?"

"Yes we are going for a week because your finals just ended." Mom said.

"Wow that's great! Can't wait!." I should win an Oscar for this acting now.

19 - Dilemmas

Zack's Pov -

I wasn't thinking, I didn't realise why I did that. I am so ashamed that I can't even think straight. I kissed Savannah, I dont know what came to me and why did I do so, I never intended to do so. She must hate me right now.

I just kissed her left without any explanation whatsoever. Few seconds ruined the friendship we have had since the past ten years. I am and always have been too scared to lose her. She is one of the most important people in my life and because I have some weird mixed feelings about her I might have most something which I dreaded to lose the most.

I don't know why did I get jealous of that Kendall . I never had a problem when Savannah blabbed about him all day when she liked her when she was in the sixth grade.

But when I saw her today with his so called date with Kendall, who may be his boyfriend, okay is his boyfriend it really did bother me. It never happened before, maybe because she never was into any guy before accept him or maybe she never had a boyfriend before.

I never used to get insecure with her making new friends specially guy friends,but today ut tinges a little bit. Am I that insecur to lose her?

Am I jealous?

Do I happen to have feelin--

No.

That can't happen under ANY circumstances.

But still one thing is yet to figure out.

Why would she kiss me back?

Usually in dilemmas like this I would, without any hesitation call sav, but in this situation I couldn't call her but I knew who to call, so I dailed brian up.

"Hey bro whatsup?"

"You still have my number Zack? That's a shocker."

"Look I know the way we met we weren't supposed to meet like that but it doesn't change the fact that you are my best friend. I deliberately need your advice."

"Sure buddy whatsup?"

I started from the top and told him the whole story,I didn't stop myself from hiding anything from him. It's weird even though we had minimal contact these years we still hit it off.

"So that's my story/ problem . What do I do?"

"I only have to ask one question Zack, do you like Savannah?"

"I-- um no maybe, maybe not. I don't know the answer to this question."

"Why did you kiss her?"

"She kissed me back."

"Dumbfuck why did YOU kiss her?"

"It was an impulse."

"Impulse to what?"

"Something I don't know."

"It's called jealousy in human language."

"Who would I be jealous of? I am Zack Ryder."

"Stick your pride in your ass please. I am gonna go talk to savs, after she was always like a sister to me."

"Yes okay."

"Hey and listen Ryder."

"What?"

"Don't hurt her because you haven't figured out your feelings."

"I would never."

Pov ends.

Just a month ago things were so much easier, no confused feelings, no second thoughts and now it's like the world is upside down. Well nothing Klaus mikaelson and Damon Salvatore can't heal.

I told this to myself as I heard a knock on the door. I am too lazy to get up at this moment know. Yes I know it's to lazy but I am a teenager gimme a break.

I opened the door and saw Brian standing with a packet of my favourite chocolates, Lindor and Ferrero Rocher. To be honest I could have expected Harry Potter in front of me but not Brian. Since he and riles broke up he never looked back and never contacted me . I knew him since he was a kid, we grew up together and was like my brother.

My aunt is a renowned councellor of our town, brian was one if her many patients . Brian had suffered more than anyone I know of my age. His grandfather whom he was very very close too died when Brian was 11 , and Zack being a kid whose parents were mostly out of town due to business saw his grandfather like his own father. He admired him, loved him, idolized him. His death made his world crumble and he couldn't focus on his studies for a whole year.

He is a year elder than me,riley and Zack but due to his mental health he dropped a year. Through my aunt my family got to know about him, we became quick friends, he was like the elder brother I had always wanted, he was very down to earth, trust worthy, funny. Though he was broken inside due to his past , he never let anyone see him as a vulnerable person.

Soon I introduced him to riley, they were both alike in many ways. I always used to ship them. Riley didn't think he was her type at first, but Brian had liked her since the first day and never gave up on her.

"Hey how are you savs?" Brian asked.

"Why are you here? Finally remember me?" I asked, well I was rather rude.

"Hey I am really sorry. I never meant to leave like I did. I was way too burdened by the break up . I never meant to hurt you, you know that. After all I had been through you and riley had been my greatest support and the thought of losing you both scared me."

"So you left without mending things?"

"I couldn't mend something if I was broken. "

I could see that he was hurt and genuinely sorry for what he did. After all I did miss him, I woukd be lying if I say I didn't. So I embraced him into a hug and he hugged me back. I am pretty sure we both were in tears. Happy tears.

I welcomed him Inside, made us some of that cup noodles because I am a terrible cook. So I couldn't risk his life with my cooking skills. We both sat,ate and talked and talked and talked.

Suddenly talking to him calmed me I felt good, like a weight was lifted off my chest. He told what all he had done the whole he wasn't here,how he dealt with his emotions and how he made himself strong enough to come back and win riley again.

I told him how confused my life got in a matter of days, how I was hanging between two guys, not sure what I felt for them or how they felt for me.

"So you are telling me that you fake dated Kendall to make Zack jealous?" He asked.

"Well not jealous, more like I was feeling betrayed." I answered.

"But all the time you spent with Kendall how did that seem?" He questioned.

"It was all real, all our laughs,talks everything was real. We didn't put and extra effort neither it seemed like we were forcing ourselves to do something for a completely vague reason." I said.

"Now you don't know what is going on?" He asked

"No clue." My face dropped.

Brian pulled me closer to him so that me head was leaning on his shoulder and he put he rested his head on my head and said,

"Hey savs chill okay, everything is gonna be okay. You will figure it out." He said consoling me .

"Yeah thanks Brian." I gave him a weak smile.

"Well now may not be the best time to tell you this but from what we have talked I know one thing." He said.

"What's that?" I asked.

"You like Kendall Parker."

***

Woohoooo , I am backkk! Ugh eleventh is tiring. Specially when you have to focus on your phone to study. I thought it'd be more fun

But how do you like Brian Adams??? He is such a sweetheart! I definitely need a friend like him in my life.

Next chapter onwards you will se more of #rilan #zacannah and #sanny.

Even I can't wait

20 - No offense

"What the hell are you staying? I can't like Ken! I mean I did like him but at that time I was 11 and I thought wizards were real. I was just a kid at that time." I almost screamed.

"Woah sav, first of all, you gotta chill! No matter how old you were you still did like him,feelings aren't wrong at any age." Brian explained.

"But I like Zack,I really do like him." I said in a rather low tone.

"I never said you didn't like him,I am just saying that you also have feelings for Kendall." He stated.

"How can I like two guys at the same time? Like it's not possible,is it?"

"It is possible sav,there is nothing wrong with it. You aren't cheating on them."

"How are you so sure I like him? What are you? A mind reader?" I asked him.

"Oh my god you won't listen to me. Um okay so when Kendall asked you on a date why did you say yes?"

"Because Zack was there and I wanted to make jealous."

"Did he get jealous?"

"No."

"So why did you get all dolled up and pretty for the date? You could have cancelled if you thought Zack wasn't jealous?" He asked.

"Um I thought it would be rude if i cancelled." I said.

"If you didn't date for real the it would not have affected anything right?" He asked raising an eyebrow.

"I don't know."

"You do."

"No I don't."

"Just say it."

"I have nothing to say."

"Savvy savvy just say."

"Only Ken calls me that."

"Oh possessive are we? Savannah Orlove just say it."

"Okay fine! I wanted to spend time with him and he was my first crush and I had always dreamt of having my first date with him. Plus not to mention he makes me happy and makes me forget about Zack." I vented out.

Oh my fucking god. What did I just say? Is it really how I feel? I mean I know somewhere it is true but how does ken have this effect on me? I never realised it. Until now.

"I didn't expect the end to be very honest." He said surprised.

"Ugh what do I do? I like two guys! what does that make me? Confused neurotic bitch?"

A slut?

Ofcourse not a slut. I said to myself.

"It makes you human, Savannah." He said looking at me with a comforting smile.

***

After a long silence, I spoke up.

"How did you do it?"I asked

"What?" He said.

"Figure that you only want to be with riley and all along she is the only one you loved even though you were not here?" I asked.

He took a deep breath looked at the sky full of stars, smiled a bit and looked at me and said.

" I always loved her, I guess I never stopped. When the person who you are with makes you forget what all have you been through,your fears,the things that upset you. The person with whom time passes away like seconds,the person is your friend, your partner,your teacher,your happy place,your counsellor and your home."

"How and when did you start feeling this?"I asked.

"By just spending time with her. You will also know it when the person comes in your life." He said.

"Why did you cheat on her?"

Yes I know I wasn't the right person to ask this but she is my best friend and I wanted to know

"I never did. That night shiela the girl who obsessed over me since elementary school took Riley's phone."

"Wait wait. I cut in. Her phone was lost before that right?" I asked.

"Turns out shiela had it all along,she texted me that night saying that riley found the phone and wanted to me to meet her in Riley's room. As she had riley's phone I thought it was her and so I went to the room. When I reached shiela was drunk as hell she practically fell over me and said she really liked me and she knew I did too and then she started forcing herself on me and as I was pushing her away, she kissed me and that's when you both entered."

"Oh my god, is that why shiela left school as you did?" I asked

"I don't know, after the breakup the months were blur."

"I am so sorry! I thought wrong about you and to make up for it I will talk to riley and tell her the whole story because currently she kinda does hate you for sabotaging her date."

"You will? Thank you so much savvvvv!!! You are the bestttt." He hugged me like a kid got his favourite toy.

***

Next day

Well what a morning! Today I have so much to do. I have to meet up with Zack and talk out about the kiss. I have to talk to Kendall too and if I have the courage to tell him about me feelings.

Most importantly I have to talk to riley.

So I went down the hallway,not knowing who I would have to face first. As I was walking first I met my history teacher, Mr. Bennet.

Well totally out of the blue.

I wished him morning and then went to the library . As I was there I spotted Zack.

Bingo.

I went up to him, wishing we don't get awkward.

"Hey Zack, can we talk?"

"Yeah okay." He said reluctantly.

"Look I know it been weird sin--"

Before I could say he cut in and said,"Yes I know it's been weird, hear me out first, so that you don't get the wrong idea."

"Wrong idea about what?"

"About us,this whatever happened that kiss."

I continued, " yes I know , I know that kiss."

Zack said,"It was the biggest mistake I made Savannah."

———————————————————————

Ouch ouch !! Did he really say that? Zack did say that!!! I know you would hate him right now.

I don't have much to say because I gotta go study

something is coming your way:)

Hey hey! First of all no this in NOT an update, though I have a very nice storyline in my head to continue this story with.

First of all thank you for your support . Almost at 2k reads!! Yippee!!

Well now I will answer the question you have in your mind "why the hell did she post this if this isn't an update?" Haha feeling's Mutual.

So as you know the title of this story is 'falling for my best friend' Obvious duh. .

Well here Savannah Orlove aka Selena Gomez has TWO best friends, Zack Ryder and Kendall Parker, right?

Oooohhhh

Please tell you get the hint *pouty face*

Well if you do great!!!

If you don't then here it goes-

As sav has two best friends which means she will fall for one of them.It can be Zack or Kendall, so if you think that Savannah and Zack could and could not be the endgame, it might be savannah and Kendall.

BUT!

It depends on you who gets to be the endgame, if Zack gets more support it will be him,if Kendall gets more support it would be him.

If I don't get enough responses by the end of the story, then it depends on me;). Hope we cool?

Plus you would have a fair share of choosing as both the guys will get equal time with savvy.

So bbye loves. I hope you like the story till now:) I really could not be more thankful<3

21- Letting it all out

Hey loves! Ik it's been long but this chapter is gonna be worth it! You all are gonna live sav's new side today (atleast I hope you do!)

***

Kendall's POV-

It's been long since I have talked to savvy or be with her,being with her also just feels perfect. Here I was wandering in the school hallway and them someone tugged my arm. I turned and to my surprise it was riley.

"Hey I know we don't really like know each other but you are Anna's good friend or boyfriend or whatever do you know where she is?"

I chuckled a bit at her straight forwardness. I replied, "I don't know where she is I am looking for her too."

While we were talking I saw Savannah rush to the girl's room and she was crying.

Wait! She is crying what the fuck?! I will kill the person who made her cry!

Riley quickly followed her and I did too, I know I couldn't go inside the girl's room but savvy was hurt I couldn't let her be alone.

"Hey ,hey Anna what happened please talk to me. Tell me what happened don't cry,love." Riley asked her while caressing her back.

She was crying bad,but in between her breaths she managed to say, "It's Zack." My jaws clenched, that bastard does nothing but hurt her,and an amazing person like her is crying because of that asshole.

"I am going to fucking kill him! " I blurted out , as I was about to walk out riley said , " hey stop you crazy pants! First let her tell what did he do before you go on your killing spree!"

"Fine,I said . I sat down, held savvy's hand and asked her what had actually happened. She started ," I wanted to talk to him about the kiss that happened and he said it was the biggest mistake of his life."

I hand turned into a fist when she mentioned her kiss, I didn't show it but I was burning inside, not jealousy but hatred for that spider. How could he say something like that? No girl deserves that. What is her fault? That she had a little crush on him? As much I hated to accept that, it was the truth I couldn't deny that but it certainly did not mean I would stop whatever I felt for her or get her to be mine.

She deserves much better. So I stood up while riley was consoling her and just as I was about to go I was stopped again. Wow .

"No ken, you won't go. You don't have to do anything because he hurt me." Savvy said.

"But you are crying because of him! He doesn't get to treat you like that,he should have a taste of what he has done."

"And he will have a taste." Savvy said.

I was officially confused. I never saw her like this. "He hurt my feelings? Guess what he doesn't deserve me. He thinks kissing me was the biggest mistake of his life? Liking him was the biggest mistake of my life. He need to hear a piece of my mind." Savvy said while wiping her tears.

"Woah easy there tiger, are you sure about this? Riley asked ,"it would ruin your friendship."

"Well I know it would but I know I can't just sit here and cry for a guy. After all I need to tell him what he did to me and we are best friends right? He deserves to know this."

Okay wow, I was shocked when I saw here being all this confident and standing up for herself. I was startled, she sure did stand up for her friends before but all this new confidence just made me like her even more. My girl never fails to amuse me.

Savannah got up, wiped her tears, fixed her, turned and gave us that evel sarcastic smile.

Oh she is hot.

"I am proud of you b!" Riley shouted and hugged her. So I was about to leave when riley stopped me.

Again.

"Okay this is the third time you stopped me from going out of the washroom, please can I go out." I begged her.

"Hey no! You and I aren't done talking ken doll." She said.

"Ken dOll? Seriously Pemberton ?"

"Yes doll sit down here I need to talk."

"Okay ma'am."

"Since when do you like anna?"

How the fuck does she know?

"How do you know?"

"Oh please I can suspect young love anywhere and I am not stupid, it's obvious."

"Well considering your past relationships I beg to differ." I laugjed a bit.

Shit should not have said so.

"Sorry I wasn't supposed to say that."

"No parki it's okay don't sweat."

"How many nicknames?"

" Yes it Pretty simple, you surname Parker so parki. That's not important right now, tell me how and why and since when do you like me best friend?"

So I told her that whole story,starting from the camp to her leaving and me not dating anyone else and the fake dating.

"All these years and you still like her?"She asked.

"How could I not she is perfect. Like I have never met such a kind, genuine, happy, caring person. After what I saw today I have never met another stronger and confident person too."

"Oh my god parki."

"What Pemberton?"

"You are in love with Savannah."

"Yes I am damn sure I am."

Pov ends

Savannah pov

I stormed out of the washroom gathered all the courage I had and went to library to find Zack. I finally spotted him in a corner reading some book.

What the hell he never reads. This is supposed to be his listening songs spot.

Ah couldn't care less.

I walked up to him and said ,"look I know you made your point very clear but I never got to say about what happened."

"Savannah, we are done talking don't stretch this topic."

"Stretch the topic? Are you out of your mind? Zachary Ryder! Yes I called you by your real name right now, first of all you kissed me out of no where when I was on a date! You pulled me out of there for no absolute fucking reason! Oh no wait, you said it was a 'family emergency'. Good at Lies too huh? Listen you don't get to play with my feelings? You know I thought I liked you! I really did but then you playing with my feelings? It hurts! I never thought that you would be the one to do that! 11 years of friendship and you can't manage to care about me feelings? "

I stopped for a bit to catch my breath I could see the emotions in his eyes.

Hurt.

Realisation.

Sad.

Shock.

"Kissing me was the biggest mistake of your life? Well liking you was the biggest mistake of my life Ryder!"

"You like me?" Zack asked, totally shocked.

Oh my god. What the hell did I just say?

***

Oh my GOD. Did sav just confess? Yes she did. YES SHE DID.

And Kendall is in love with Savannah? Oooooooohhhh

Plus I really like riley and Kendall's friendship, just to be clear no nothing will happen between them. Riley has another guy for herself;)

22- Who is she?

"You like me?" Zack asked me in disbelief.

"You are missing the bigger picture here, I 'liked' you. After what you did I can't even be around you. Who do you think you are? Some big bad playboy who gets to juggle with people's feelings? No, I won't be one of those girls. Bye Ryder." I said though I could feel that even I was hurting inside while saying so.

As I was walking away, Zack held my hand and said , " can we atleast be friends?" With a hopeful look in his eyes.

"Are you kidding me right now?" He is unbelievable. I gave him a look of disappointment, pulled my hand away and stormed out the library. I was trying my best to control my tears and not look back.

Even though we both were hurting inside, I felt like a weight was lifted off my chest. I know this isn't the best way to confess your feelings but after all the crush and feelings situation, I was getting annoyed and wanted to let it out. So it felt good and nice after confessing.

***

I went down the hallway to see Kendall and riley coming out of anatomy class,I ran towards them and lunged on to riley and said, "have I ever told you how much I love you, riles?"

"I love you,too anna banana! Now tell me what's wrong?" She asked with that 'what did you do now' face.

"I let all my feelings and annoyance to zack, it feels like a big load is of my chest . So you , me and kenny, I said entwining our hands, "are going to get ice cream after school,okay?"

They both looked at and smiled, I stood on my toes and hugged Ken and said , "I love you ,kenny."

His eyes turned warm and he blushed? Wow. He still looked cute. He put a hand on my cheek and said, "I love you,too savvy."

I pecked both of them on the cheek and literally skipped my way to the class. I think people might have thought that I have gone bonkers. On the way to my class I could only think if one thing.

How perfect it felt to be in Kendall's arms and wow he smelled like chocolate.

Zack's POV -

How come I never knew how my best friend liked me and still did this to her? I am such an insensitive freak! I couldn't stand the idea of her going out with someone else so I ruined her date, lied to her and then kissed her out of the blue! How pathetic can I be.

The rest of the day I spent in school was blur. I couldn't take my mind off of the things sav said. I could see how hurt she was, the look she had in her eyes while screaming at me,broke my heart. I wish I could turn back time and control the feelings but the thing about feelings is that you can't control them.

The way I felt for her I haven't for anyone. I don't know what am I feeling, it is wrong, I can break my friendship with her forever and I can't let that happen at any cost. I admit I have some confused feelings for her which I can't figure out, but if they hurt sav in any way it's better I crumpled whatever I felt and throw it far away.

I wanted to talk to her,even for a little while so that I can tell whatever I did was because I was jealous. I mean it's natural if your best friend goes out with someone else the fear of you being replaced is there, isn't it?

Gosh I so want to talk to her right now, she is the only one who gives great advice in every situation. Whatever happens I am sure of one thing.

I will get my sav back.

Pov ends

Ice cream parlor

Riley and I went together to the ice cream parlor and texted ken if he was about to come. He said he will bring a friend,which we were cool with as we never got to meet his friends back in his town.

As we were walking down the road , I saw a girl running and hugging a guy like they hadn't met in ages, aw cute.

It wasn't cute till I realised the guy was kenny, wait what?!

"Who the hell is she? " I asked riley.

"Seems like she is pretty close to kendoll." She said smirking.

"Yeah and we don't know about her, be never mentioned this whoever she is. How can he being her here."

Something tinged inside me when I saw them together so engrossed in talking to each other, laughing. I could see she was clinging on to him,okay who does that?

"Hey you look umm jealous anns, do you have a wittle crush on ken doll huh?" Riley asked with her baby voice.

Yes.

What?

Yes?

No.

No?

Yes?

Ughhh

"No I am just curious okay?" I sais in a rather harsh tone.

I couldn't help but notice one thing. They looked happy.

———————————

Ooooooohhhh who is the mystery girllll?? Any guesses?;))

23 - Meeting the ex

"Who is she?" I asked riley.

"Guess we will have to go there and find out." She replied like she knew something which made me more curious.

Riley and I went there, I could already see Kendall's beaming smile while talking to her gosh he looks so cute. They both were talking like it had been ages since they had mat, it wasn't late till I saw the girl's face. She had blonde hair, deep blue eyes, a perfect makeup no makeup look. She looked like a barbie had come to life, she had a very pretty smile. Looks like a typical mean bitch.

"Hey savvy!" Kendall cam and hugged me and riley, " meet Loren a friend from back home, Loren meet Savannah and riley ."

A friend? Liar

"She doesn't seem like just a friend to me." I snickered.

"Yes Kendall I am not just a friend! I am his ex girlfriend too." She said and linked her arms with Ken.

Hey hey you are his ex in your limits.

"Well Kendall talked about you a lot back in town! You are prettier in person." She said and hugged me.

Okay either she is buttering me up or she is genuinely nice.

Buttering up.

Nice person.

Buttterrrinnggg upp.

Don't judge so quick, she is nice, must be nice.

She dated Kendall

Okay she is buttering up.

"Hey hey hey don't get all judgey okay? We have to go get ice cream." Riley said while pulling me with her hands.

"Don't be so obvious anna." She whispered.

"About what ?"

"Please if we stayed any longer you would have burnt the girl up, you know you can just admit you like him."

"I -- what? Huh-- Kendall? My ken? My best friend? I don't like him." I scoff.

"Yes sure you don't darling. Keep telling yourself that." Riley winked at me and went inside the shop.

Flashback

Kendall's POV (school hallway)

"Well she seems very happy." I said to riley.

"She just hit a milestone by standing up to zack who is her 'crush.'" she said while teasing me on purpose to make me jealous.

"What does she even see in him? He isn't even nice to her, I mean she should definitely go for someone else." I said.

"Oh you mean she should go for you?" Riley replied.

"Ofcourse she should go for me, I will rip apart if someone else gets in between." I said with a smirk.

"Okay parki I want to tell you something." Riley said seriously.

"I know for a fact that she has feelings for you, I mean I know she would kill me if I say this but you were her crush. She literally was in love with you throughout the middle school. The reason I am telling you this is because you both are made for each other and Zack is kind of a playboy and is confused about his feelings and I don't want her to get hurt. I know she still has feelings for you but doesn't realise it right now, you need to give her a push. "

Whatever riley just said was spinning my head, the girl I was in love with had feelings for me? I was so dumb to figure it out over all the jealousy . I couldn't help but smile at the thought of us together. We both liked each other in the middle school until they Ryder came in between. Well now I know for a fact what I have to do to get my savvy.

"I know how to give her a push." I said to riley.

"Okay spill, I am all in. Just don't go overboard." She said.

"So there is this girl loren, we used to date in middle school it didn't last because I didn't feel that much for her. We did end on good terms and we still are friends and she is staying at her aunt's house nearby, what if I invite her today to the ice cream shop we all are going?" I said.

"This definitely sounds like a plan but are you sure she doesn't like you or wants you back? Things could get messy." She asked.

"She won't have feelings for me she has been dating this girl named Kiara for the past 7-8 months and she is perfectly happy and I would never bring someone who could create problems between me and savvy." I said

"Well then this sounds perfect! You are smart kendoll. Is it because if my influence?"She said with sarcasm.

"Oh my god what would I have done without you Pemberton!!" I reply with a fake gasp.

Flashback ends.

We all sat down and I deliberately sat next to loren to see savvy's reaction. We ordered our Ice Cream . Savannah ordered for a triple chocolate fudge, riley and loren ordered a sundae and I got Belgium chocolate.

I could see savvy did not like loren from the beginning it was mine and Loren's plan to act like our old memories have been rekindled to see her reaction. I had already filled loren about Savvy and even she had started shipping us which I obviously loved.

Today Savvy was wearing a black lace crop top with high waist blue jeans and a crescent moon necklace and black high tops. She had her hair in a fish braid. She looked beautiful. She always does.

God how can someone be so perfect.

Pov ends.

"So when did you come back in town loren?" I asked her curiously.

More like why was she here.

"Oh just a week ago to meet my aunt." She said.

"How did you and kendall meet? Considering he never told me about you."
I said giving Kendall a slight smile .

"We had mutuals actually and they said that we would look cute together
and we git to know each other better and then he asked me out and then
asked me to be his girlfriend,you know the normal." She said

"Oh why did you break up,if you don't mind me asking." I said.

Yes okay! I was a bit jealous I mean Kendall never even mentioned having
a girlfriend. What if he still liked her and she took him away from me and
they live happily ever after and he forgets me.

Wow I am a drama queen.

Riley hit my leg from below the table and giving me the 'what the hell are
you doing look' I could see that Kendall was Chuckling while eating his
ice cream . What is he upto?

"You know I really don't remember what happened that we broke up. I am
just happy that I got to meet kenny again." She smiled and winked at him.

"I mean kenny and I have so much history together it's hard to ignore I
mean we go way back and he used to make me so happy." She then kept his
arm around him.

Oh no.

She did not just call him kenny !

How the fuck she? How does she not know only I call him that?

Well if she was so happy they didn't have to break up.

Oh god this loren is so so so annoying!

"You two deem to be enjoying yourself, I think riley and I should leave considering you two are very 'happy' with each other aren't you?" I said irritated.

I got up took Riley be the hand and said, "bye Kendall, see you at school."

And left the shop with her

***

I know this is not that good of a chapter but lot is coming soon!!! More #sanny.

And know I haven't forgotten Zack! I have something planned for #zacannah too and it's coming very soon like maybe in the next two chapters:)

25 - Feelings can't be hidden

"Where do you think you are going?" Riley screamed.

"Giving Kendall and his barbie ex some time alone, it's clear they need that!" I shouted back.

"Tell him already anna! " Riley said while stopping me by grabbing my hand.

"Tell him what?" I asked her.

"Please I know you like him, it's clear tha yoy are jealous just confess him already, marry him and have kids and then get your kids married." She said.

"Let's not go to future impossible tense. I don't like him." I replied.

"Don't lie to me,let alone yourself." She said.

"I can't like him I mean I know I was a bit harsh on Zack but I still have feelings for him and kendall--" I stopped to catch my breath.

"Kendall what?" Riley asked with and eyebrow up.

"Kendall can go and marry his ex! Remind me why are we here Even?"

"Savannah Orlove! Get your butt here! " Riley screamed.

Okay she is mad. I am gonna die.

Tell my parents I loved them, god.

"Why don't you just say it?" She asked.

"You know it, why are you asking?" I said.

"Why aren't you saying?"

"Why are you asking?"

"Saying!"

"Asking!"

"Saying!"

"Okay fine I maybe like Kendall too ! There you go happy?" I almost screamed and I am pretty sure Kendall and that barbie heard it. I looked in the shop through it glass and ken was blushing?

"Yes!! I knew you liked him!!" Riley practically jumped over me while saying so.

"Go get your man anna! I am rooting for 'sandall'! "She said.

"You want sandals in this time of crisis? " I asked her confused.

"I meant as in your couple name idiot." She laughed.

"Please find a job smiley riley,cupid isn't going well for you!"

"You love me." She smirked and left.

There I was standing, having no clue what to do, I have never been this awkwardly nervous before. I thought the best idea was to leave the place and deal with Ken later on but as I was walking, someone held my waist and turned me around , that someone was Ken.

I had no clue I stood there like frozen meat, I was very nervous by his touch. I could feel my skin erupting like my hormones were on fire, at the same time his touch made me feel calm amd protected like I had never felt before with anyone. He stood there holding me, I was gazing into his hazel eyes as sunlight fell on them. His warm brown hair looked golden as the sunrays fell on them.

Oh my god ! I would be dead if looks could kill.

"Did I hear that savvy has a crush on me?"he asked with a smirk on his face.

"Um no, I don't know what you are talking about mister." I said after pulling his hand from my waist.

Okay I did not have to do that.

"You can just confess savvy, I mean it is really cool if you have a crush on me like I would love that." He said.

"Listen Kendall, it is very confusing . It wasn't until last week I figured I had a crush on you. I thought it was for a while because you were my first ever crush. I thought it was a mere attraction, but when I saw you today getting cozy with that blond barbie I don't know what came up to me and I ran off that was very rude, I could not control that i was a but jealous of her and -- "

as I was blabbering all this I realised what Ken had said so I asked," Wait, why would you love me liking you?"

"Because then I would be able to do this--"

He smiled and leaned towards me by grabbing my waist with one hand and my check with another and he kissed me.

———————————

Okay okay what did just happen!? OMG OMG.

Is #Sanny happening? Eeeppp.

First off I know this is a short chapter, but surprise surprise? I will upload another Chapter today just for Zack's Pov.

YES A DOUBLE UPDATE!

Kidding?NO

Will I surely upload today? YES

just wait for a few hours:)

Love you guys

26 - Falling for her

Z ack's Pov-

So I had a football match today and we lost, I played horribly, I was even ashamed of myself but I couldn't help it during the whole game only one line and that one person was on my mind, "I liked you, Zack!"

Throughout the whole game I had mixed feelings, some part of me hated myself for making sav upset,some part of my was terrified of losing my best friend but the most strange feeling I had the whole day was that it felt weirdly nice when sav confessed that she had feelings for me, I don't know I just wish I could turn back time and hug her tightly and apologize to her.

Then ask her out. My subconscious said.

No,I won't ask her out.

Okay then kiss her again.

Absolutely not, if I wanted a death wish I would just let everyone know that my real name is Zachary. I was even hurt when she called me 'zachary' ,by my real name because I was the most bullied kis in the whole class in elementary school because I had the bluest eyes and people would call me alien, now girls drool all over me just because of my eyes, hypocrites.

Sav never called me Zachary , like never. The reason we were best friends because when the whole grade was teasing my for having the bluest eyes she said that my eyes were beautiful and that she loved that shade of blue, since then we had been inseparable. Way to ruin a perfectly good friendship Zack.

I came back home and slouched on the couch trying to figure out what was going inside my head, that's when dad came to the living room and said," well you look beat."

"I have had a very tough day dad, I even lost the football match." I said with my eyes fixed on the floor.

"Yeah, coach Durham called me, what happened out there son? You have never played like this." He questioned.

"It's just umm stuff you know like school and all." I said trying to avoid the topic.

" Man up and say it's about a girl." He said smiling.

"What are you a psychic dad?" I asked giving out a little chuckle.

"No I just happened to be once your age and I know that look ain't because of some 'school stuff." He said " so tell me what is this girl high school drama."

I told him everything from the start about sav,her date,me getting jealous for some unknown reason. Me kissing her, her going all 'i am so mad I could kill you' lecture at the library . Dad didn't look surprised at first but when I said that she had called me by my real name his expression changed and he had a stern look on his face that's when I realised I had fucked up, pretty bad.

"Well we know a thing for sure." Dad said.

"What is that?" I asked

"That you are an ass son." He said with a serious face and then laughed.

"What? What was I supposed to do? I don't know what came over me I just did what I did and I have no explanation for it whatsoever and I --" I trailed of for a few seconds and then realised , " oh wait, I am an ass."

"A friend like that girl Savannah is very difficult to find, she is like a daughter to me and you being her best friend could not see it through." Dad said.

"I know that dad, I cant change what happened, but I want to change what will happen I feel really guilty." I said with an apologetic tone.

"Well you should be guilty, but at the end of the day she is your best friend I am sure you know how to mend things son and you should because she made you the best person I could have ever imagined, you and I both know I am not wrong there." He said whole patting my shoulder.

"Yes dad, I think I know how to get sav back." I said confidently.

"Good son! Go and mend things with her and this time don't kiss her if you can't control your hormones." He said with a smug look on his face.

"Father of the year." I said and went out.

Whenever sav would be upset or we would have a fight the only way for us to make up for each other would be to be the triple chocolate fudge ice cream from the downtown ice cream parlour, it was a ritual for us. No matter how bad one person screwed up, if you buy the other person that ice cream you are let off the hook.

So I got my car, went to that shop while smiling to the thought that sav would forgive me and hug me and we could be past this. It was just one fight that made me realise how empty my life was without her, her laugh,her stupid jokes, her bad and sometimes good music sense , her weird and best ways to make me happy and that smile of hers,that beautiful smile.Okay what the fuck am I thinking? I can't be such a girl. I parked my car and got off and I saw the thing I dreaded the most until now.

Savannah kissing some other guy. Not just any other guy it was that son of a bitch golden boy. I swear to god I will Fucking kill him! My jaw clenched and I practically broke my car rear view mirror at the sight of this, not only she was kissing him back she looked happy.

God why does it hurt so much?I mean I should be happy she is with a guy and is happy right?

Maybe I am just protective of her.

Or you are jealous.

A good friend.

Yeah just a friend whom she won't kiss.

I am just looking out for her. He isn't the right guy for her.

And you are? My inner subconscious asks me.

Ofcourse I am!

Wait, what the hell am I saying.

I called Brian because I didn't have anyone else to call at this moment, I would call sav but she is busy making out with that golden boy of hers . I stormed of the place with my car so i could clear my head and that's when Brian picked the call up.

"Hey what's up zack?"

"What does it mean when u get jealous of a guy kissing a girl?" I ask

"Depends are you gay or straight?" He asked.

"I am straight ." I replied.

"Well then you like the girl."

This is not good.

"Hello Zack??" He said bringing me back to my senses.

"Yeah what?"

"Don't make it so obvious that you like Savannah." He said and cut the call.

Oh my god this can't be happening. I mean she is my best friend, I can't like her I mean I don't like her. I guess then I looked at her smiling and striking her hands through her Auburn hair.

Gosh I am falling for my best friend.

———————————

OH BOYYYYY!!! WHAT DID JUST HAPPEN?

HOW LONG HAVE YOU BEEN WAITING FOR THIS?

TOO LONG I KNOW!

btw what a story title reference;)

27 - Stuck

I woke up at 7 am today, considering what went down yesterday and how my day changed from being upset because I had a fight with Zack to being super awesome when Kendall kissed me, I never would have imagined a day like that. I woke up with a smile on my face, just the thought of Kendall kissing me made me blush.

I went to take a shower and get ready for school. I came out after 30 minutes, when I was drying my hair in front of my mirror, it was a picture of me and Zack on his fifth birthday in Park Avenue. It was the most perfect day for me and Zack, both. The picture could tell us, we were on a roller coaster laughing like complete idiots but we looked happy, very happy . How did everything get so complicated?

That's when I decided that no matter what, I got to make things right with Zack , I know what he did hurt my feelings but even I got mad too much and spurt out words I didn't mean, okay maybe I did but I can't entirely blame him and throw such a great friendship away he doesn't deserve this.

***

I reached school and I had history as my first period just the same as Zack. I was planning to talk to him after the class when he walks me to my locker, I meam he usually did so since the past three years. I waited for him in the class and he didn't arrive until our teacher had arrived. He walked into the class with ruffled hair,his eyes looking tired like he barely sleep. He usually sits next to me but today he came to his usual seat looked at me gave me a sad look?

What is up with him?

During the class I tried to get his attention but he won't even look at me. He changed his seats and focused on the class the whole time or out the window. That is not like him.

When the class got over I was packing my stuff and after that I tried to get ahold of Zack but he had already stormed off . I looked for him in the hallway and found that he was making out with someone skank.

Wait.

Who the fuck is he kissing?

Why is he even doing it?

Is this guy out if his freaking mind?

Who does he think he is?!

Why am I getting jealous ugh.

I muster up my courage and walked to him . I literally pulled away him from the girl he was sucking and asked him with rahe in my eyes," We need to talk. Now!"

Zack's Pov -

After watching Savannah and that golden boy together I was full of anger , I could literally rip apart that guy's throat. I had no intention of going to school today and face the both of them by now they must be all mushy and cute with each other and I do not want to witness such a thing.

When I entered the history class I could see Sav searching for me and went to sit in my usual seat she gave me a casual sweet smile and I almost forgot for a moment that she kissed someone else.

She is not even my girlfriend, why am I getting this affected?

What is her fault in all this? Liking someone?

Yes liking someone else other than me when she clearly said that she liked me!

That's not cheating but it is 'Partial cheating.'

If that's a thing.

I know the whe time she wanted to get me attention, cute. I wanted to shake my thoughts off her but I couldn't and to get her attention more I stormed off the class knowing she would follow me. I had texted a girl from the cheerleading squad earlier to 'meet up' basically a small hookup if we are digging for the meaning.

I started making out with her vigorously to get Savannah's attention I didn't enjoy the makeout sesh because I wanted to kiss Savannah and be with her not some cheerleader whose name I didn't know, I don't even want to know her name.

"We need to talk now!" She said.

"What making out is not so fun when you are not the one doing it?" I snapped back.

"What do you mean?" She asked .

God she smells like blueberries, is she using a new shampoo?

"Don't act innocent, you know what? Don't even bother asking! I gotta go." I said rather rudely.

What? I was mad and jealous.

She stopped me by holding my hand which gave me a warm fuzzy feeling. She looked at me with her warm brown eyes and said, "I know you are very mad right now, I know I said too much and you didn't deserve it . I am so sorry Zack , I am really very sorry."

Oh my god I truly hurt her and she is very sad I could see she had a droplet of year in her eyes just as I was about to clasp her hands in mine and answer her Kendall came and literally snatched her hands from mine and hugged her.

That son of a bitch!

"Hey what are you doing here?" He asked and then gave a pause , "that too with him?" He finished.

For the last part he got a death glare from me. Now that he ruined my time with her it's time for some payback.

"Oh you are here Kendall, how are you and your girlfriend doing? " I said shifting my eyes to Savannah.

"She isn't my girlfriend ye--" he was about to finish but I cut him off.

"Well that's a good thing you aren't dating yet I mean yesterday Savannah here confessed that she had feelings for me." I said giving him a playful smirk.

"Zack what are you saying?!" Sav said.

"What the hell are you talking about?"Kendall shouted.

"Ooh and yeah not only that remember when you were on your little date? I took Savannah home and we kissed it's a good thing you aren't dating you know."

"Ryder are you out of your mind!" Savannah screamed at me.

Okay I went too overboard here I guess. I could see that sav could kill me any moment right now and I saw how hurt she was looking like I had betrayed it. I realised that I sounded like a total jealous asshole. Fuck. Before I could say anything else Kendal said,

"Is it true savvy? You kissed him?"

"Kenny its just that when we wen--." She was explaining but Kendal asked again.

"Did you or did you not kiss him Savannah?" He asked with more determination and looked a hell of a lot more angry and disappointed.

Savannah looked at me with tears in her eyes and muttered , "Yes, we kissed."

"Wow, just wow Savannah I-- can't believe, you know what? If you both have a thing for each other go for it but you lost me today Savannah, you lost me." Kendall said and stormed off and punched the locker nearest to him leaving a bit of a dent.

I looked at Savannah, before I could apologize she shouted on the top of her lungs,

"You son of a bitch Ryder! What were you thinking you jackass?!"

OOOOHHH DRAMA

We love a drama right?I do!

I really enjoyed this chapter,I am a very sadistic person ig:)

PS - I am watching riverdale and jughead's little sister's name is jellybean I mean wow

28 - Riley to the rescue

After Ken left the hallway no one had heard from him, where he went, how he was? I hated myself for this because I knew I was the reason he left school in the middle of the day. I had pissed him off, kind of cheated on him? I don't should I call it that? I mean we weren't dating dating, but I had feelings for him I was just stupid enough to realise it after this whole fiasco. The only thing that I couldn't understand is that why did Zack even do something like this?

A part of me wanted to hate and wanted to rip his throat apart for what he said, another part of me wanted to confront him that why he did what he did. Deep down I knew whatever he said wasn't a lie and even though I know I could have told Kendall the truth before, I just couldn't I don't know why but I couldn't. Even now I want to say everything that happened from the beginning to Ken but I just can't find the words for it, I am scared to face him now I really thinks he hates me.

Way to mess up Orlove, big time!

The whole day of school went by as a blur, Zack was no where to be seen, Kendall was MIA and my beloved best friend was at a music competition, great just when I need her the most!

I went home witha really crappy mood I just wanted to hit something or throw something or break something I mean anything! I reached home and opened the door with a loud thud and my mom came running.

"Savannah Perkins Orlove! Are you trying to break the door?"

"Mom I am not really in the mood right now!" I shouted back.

"Seriously what hap-- oh sweetie have u been crying? Are you okay baby?" She asked with concern

"I have not been crying I am just flushed with anger I don't know what is going on mom! I don't know how to fix it either I feel so numb right now." I said with a puddle forming in my eyes.

"Oh kiddo come here." My mom said whole pulling me into a hug "what happened? Talk to me."

That's when I looked at mom and start blabbering everything from the beginning, that dare, my crush on Zack , Kendall showing up,fake date everything. After 20 minutes I stopped and looked at her. She looked um amazed? I guess.

"You have so much drama in your life! I swear to god I will exchange your life drama for one tree hill's drama." She said while laughing.

"Moooooommmmmmmm! Not the time please as much as I would like a one tree hill marathon again, it's not the time!" I whined like a five year old kid.

"Fine fine okay! So tell me how can u help you anna?" She asked

"How would you know who you like if you were confused between two guys?"

"Um well kiddo I have two theories, but they are totally opposite wanna hear?" She asked and I nodded my head.

"First is that, when you like someone, and you get feelings for another guy during that time,go for the second one because if you really iked the first one you wouldn't have had feelings for the second." She said.

"That is ... Umm..... Not wrong. Yeah it makes sense. So should I go for Kendall?" I asked.

"Firstly kid, I won't tell who you have to go fir it's your job to decide and hear out my second theory okay?" To which I said ,"okay."

"Well when you like two guys, the second guy only comes in your life to make you realise how much you need and want the first one in your life."she said

"Mom we are back to square one! This isn't helping!" I said.

"I know but these do make sense, very much and which on you apply is on you and just to be clear there is one of the guys in your room now." She said while patting my shoulder.

"What? No! Not happening I am not ready to face them at this moment! Please just 'shu' them away,you know like we shu little pigeons away? Pwweease mommyyy" I said whole pouting my lips.

"Haha kiddo! Not happening! Go solve up this mess now go shu kiddo." She said.

Oh my god! My own mother 'shued' me that so not done! Guys are jerks.

I went up the stairs slowly,very slowly,like if I was about to get shot if I reach up there. I was not sure who was it, Zack or Ken. At this moment I would be glad if I had Klaus mikealson in my room saying "sorry love, but I am here to take you to New Orleans."

I would have gladly joined him even if I had to walk

I peeped through me door and looked inside that I wasn't gonna meet a psychopath inside. I opened the door and there he was, Zack.

"Sav please listen before kicking me out just listen to me let me apologize and just hear me out I have a --." He stopped.

"Hey why aren't you answering?" He asked.

"No just go ahed with your apology you pompous dick!" I screamed

"Language Savannah!!" My mom shouted from the living room

Wow moms.

"Savannah I get you are very mad at me but I have a very good reason behind it please just don't hate me for it." He said with pleading eyes.

"Fine, spill."

"Savannah I did this because..... Ummm I --" he paused.

" You what?"

"Sav it's just that i -"

"If you don't say it I will." We heard a voice from behind and guess who it was! Yess riley is here!

"Thank god you are here riles!" I squealed and hugged her.

"Seriously I go for one music competition and I miss all the love triangle drama." She said will bouncing off to the sofa.

"Wait you know?" Zack and I asked in unison.

"Yes ofcourse I do! The whole school is talking about it, if you don't fess up right now,hero hair I will and that won't be pretty." She said whole eyeing to zack.

"Yeah just tell zack!" I said.

"I was jealous." He said in a low tone.

"What?" I asked "why?" I asked again.

"Because I have feelings for you sav, I really like you." He said whole looking at me .

"You what now?" I asked in disbelief.

"Yes DRAMA!" Riley said while jumping on my bed.

"You like me? When? How? Why? " For the first time this had happened the guy I liked has liked me back and that to is my best friend! My best freaking friend! Is this for real or am I in a teenage rom com?

"I don't know it just happened when you started going out with Ken I thought I would be cool but I wasn't soon I thought I was just being a good best friend but then you went on a date with him looking like a perfect angel I could not stop myself and I realised how jealous I was that's why I kissed you and wanted you to not be on a date with him and then I saw you both kissing in front of our ice cream place and I just lost it and that's why I acted out today sav, I really really like you I don't know how but you are just something else sav I don't know what to do without you." He said and took my and hands in his.

"I swear I think I am in a Wattpad story! But now that you have confessed your work is done here baby blue eyes (Zack) go and apologize to Kendall and explain him everything while I come up with a plan to solve this messed up love equation.'" Riley said as she separated me and Zack.

"I am not apologizing to that ass! He can do whatever he wants I don't care." He said with an angry voice.

"Zack it's your fault Kendall and sav are not speaking right now even though you said the truth it wasn't your place to do so just fix things with him just don't kill each other okay? Toodles hero hair!!" She said while pulling Zack out the door and slamming the door in hai face.

Ooh I liked that.

"Now you have riley to the rescue and I have the perfect plan so that you can figure out what your out of control teenage hormones want peaches." Riley said as she winked at me.

Oh god this can't be good.

———————————————

Oh em geeeeee ZACK CONFESSED!

WHAT WILL HAPPEN NOW?

and don't you just love riley? Coz I do! She is amazing!!

But waitttt

What is her plan! Huh?

29 - The plan

Riley took a deep breath and stared me for quite a bit. I was getting anxious not because of the look she gave me but because of her, her plans are well, um not so healthy? Like they work most of the time but the risk percentage is high.

"You need to be their girlfriend for one day each." She said with a very serious tone.

" I what now?" I asked her in complete shock.

"You heard me, you have to date or go one a date and be Zack and Kendall's girlfriend for a whole day, you know like those YouTube challenges?" She said.

"Are you serious right now riley?" Ofcourse she is, she just called Zack and Kendall by their names instead of a nickname.

"Do I look like I am kidding peaches? Trust me it's the only way you could figure out which boy-toy you want."

"This is a crazy plan!" I silently screamed.

"What is a crazy plan?" I turned around to see that Zack and ken were on the door.

"Hey look your boy toys are here!" Riley said with fake joy.

"Okay what is going on? How did you two makeup so quick?" I asked Zack and ken.

"Well, this guy right here apologized for being a jealous dick which I understood because I might have done the same, just in a much better way." Ken said and winked at me.

"Okay I deserve that but this apology? Was a one time thing don't get over your head." Zack said.

"Gosh you fight like girls, sorry peaches your girl toys are here." Riley said with a devil smile.

"So what plan were you talking about?" Kendall asked riley and me

"To be honest my best friend riley, is out of her mind right now, she is suggesting bad ideas like confetti." I said whilst giving riley a stern look

"Cool down, PMS. It is a very rational plan, you just have to be both of their girlfriends for a day and decide which boy toy you want. Simple. " She said while giving us the most adorable smile.

"Excuse me? Blondie are you out of your little brain?" Zack said while shooting daggers from his eyes.

"Blondie? This is the best you could come up with?" Riley said

"Well it makes sense because um you are .... Blond." Zack said giving an obvious look

"You have brown hair, do I call you brownie? No, because brownies are awesome and well you are, you. I don't know why sav liked you in a first place. " Riley said giving a sarcastic smile.

"Thanks for the encouragement blonde bitch." Zack said and threw you pillow at her.

Now you must be wondering that why are they fighting so much? Well Zack and riley are cousins, well half cousins. Zack's aunt married riley's dad when riley was four, they were forced to be friends. Though they love each other, I guess. They bicker a lot,one of the reasons is that In grade school Zack had to wear baby blue socks , well riley forced him to so that it could match his eyes, hence the name baby blue eyes comes. Since then Zack has always wanted revenge but riley always outsmarted him. Second reason is that Zack is best friends with riley ex Brian.

Wait.

Oh my god.

How could I forget?

Brian!

I know how to get back at riley if I accept this plan of hers now.

"I think it's a good idea." Kendall said after staying silent for a ling time. We all looked at him with different looks not sure why he said so.

"Look savvy, I have waited for you for a very long time now, almost like ten years? From summer camp to grade school high school and now I am a senior. All this while you are the only girl I have ever lov-- liked. It would suck to see you for Zack's girlfriend but he deserves an equal chance here and if this helps to figure you out who you want I am all in." Ken said with an understanding smile on his face.

"For once I don't find your buttface not so annoying." Zack said .

"Wish I could say tha same Ryder." Ken said with a sarcastic tone.

Wow they are back at it again. Jerks.

"Well my job here is done I gotta go figure this love triangle okay? Toodles!" Riley said and as she was going to bail on us that's when I stopped her and said

"I will only do this if you give Brian another chance." I said which made riley turn.

"You have got to be kidding me, I will never give that cheating son of a bitch a second chance." Riley said with anger in her eyes

"He didn't cheat on you riles."

"What do you mean?"

That's when I told her what Brian had said to me the day he came to my house. I told her that at that party the girl just lunged onto him and texted him from Riley's phone to meet up. The girl tricked Brian into meeting her up and at the end I said, " after all this he came back for you, to get you back, he is still in love with you riley."

"He is?" She gulped as puddles of water were forming in her eyes like she could break down any second. No matter how tough and funny she might be on the outside but I side she is a real sweetheart and the most caring person I know. She just doesn't let her guard down so that she doesn't get hurt like she was two years ago.

"That asshole could not have said this to my face?" Riley said with anger. Okay she is back wow.

"You know what I am just gonna tell him to move on with one of the many girls I hangs out with at school. It must be easy right? For him now that he came back ten times hotter from that army school." She said with a hint of jealousy in her voice.

"Hey you are jealous."I said and smirked

"Jealous and me? Ha no! I am just gonna help him find the perfect girl for him." Riley said

"Oh you mean yoy are gonna introduce him to yourself blondie?" Zack said in between.

"You know that I still don't like you right 'brownie' ." She said with air quotes.

"What if he turns out gay?" Kendall said to tease riley.

"Well then I will kindly offer him to go out with the guy who my best friend, anna Orlove leave heartbroken between the two of you." She said and gave us a wink.

"Wow she is good." Kendall said to which Zack and I 'hmmed'.

Now there was silence, I decided to break it and said

"So how are we gonna do this date thing?"

———————————————

Wooohooooo! How is the plan? The next two chapters will have many zacannah and kevannah scenes!!

Yeah I changed sanny to kevannah, how is it?

Till we meet again! Toodles <3

30 - shocking revelation

Hey guys first off this is a chapter, but not a big one. When I was reading the last chapter I realised I missed something very important and without it the story wouldn't make sense. While writing the last chapter I forgot it sowie:(

This is gonna be a short chapter because I wanted to give one whole chapters for the dates of Zacannah and Kennah as sav will be spending a whole day with each one if them as their girlfriend. Plus I would really like if yoy wanted to pitch in some idea for her dates with our boys. So you can comment or text me privately if you want to give some ideas and if I like it I would use it in the story and I will give creds to the people' who give ideas :) and yes the next chapter, the first date will come this weekend!! Ps- it will be a long one;)

Now I was getting ready for my first date today, which was with Zack. A smile crept in my face when I thought of Zack and I spending the whole day together like a real couple after my school girl crush on him. I had always spent time with him as a friend but not as a girlfriend. Even though I was excited to spend the whole day with Zack the thought of what kenny said to me before he left yesterday lingered in my head.

Flashback

"So how should we do it?" I asked looking at both of them.

"You have to go one dates with each of us and spend a whe day being our girlfriend." Zack said.

"Wow I sound like a playgirl." I said and chuckled

"Well who would you like to go with as your first date?" Kendall asked me with hopeful eyes

I didn't know the answer to this question because ofcourse, if a chose the guy I want go with as my first date it would be clear who I would choose between the two of them and this question was the only thing that troubled me.

"Let's do head and tails." Zack suggested.

"What are you mad?" Ken snickered.

"Or do you wanna go with rock, paper and scissors,golden boy?" Zack replied back

"Um I think the toss is better." I suggested.

"Fine I take heads you take tails, the person that wins gets the first date." Zack said and took out a coin from his letterman jacket's pocket.

Ken took the coin and gave it to me to toss it, I was a bit worried not because I had to choose and who was I gonna go with but I didn't know I could toss a coin.

Anyway I tossed it and it came out to be heads, which meant my first date was with Zack.

"Well well, anna I guess you are my girlfriend then." Zack said as he slinged his hand on my shoulder and winked at me wish made me blush

"It just for one day jack ass." Ken said as he shoved his hand from my shoulder and held my hand and said, "no worries I will make your second date worth it,babe.

When he called me babe my cheeks were flushed with heat,first he has this hot raspy voice which anyone would die for and second it just felt so,perfect

"Don't babe her,Goldie you aren't his boyfriend." Zack said in a harsh tone

"Not yet." Ken said with a new confidence and rubbed his thumb over my hand.

I was in a weird situation so I moved away from the both if them and said, "so it's settled first date Zack,second ken and you two will make plans don't leave it on me okay?"

They both nodded to this and went for the front door Zack left in his car but before that he hugged me and said ,"be ready for tomorrow,pretty girl." While stroking my cheek which sent shivers down my spine and I blushed, I could see a pair of eyes glaring at me and Zack , ken.

"I need to talk savvy." Ken said

"Yea what's up?" I asked

"Look I know you have a date with him tomorrow, and it's cool but I need you to know this. I just don't want to pressure you but it's important for you to know this. Don't hate me after this." Ken said.

"Kenny, my drama queen, just say it I won't hate you."

"If you choose Zack after both the dates and not me just know that I have waited for you too long and if you two are together in front of me I won't be here to see it. Heck I can't even bear to imagine it."

My heart skipped a beat when he said so what does he mean he won't be here?

"What do you mean?" I amsed him.

"If you choose Zack, I will leave this town and won't come back here, ever again Savannah." He said and let out a sigh.

31 - The First Date (part 1)

" **A**re you ready for your date pretty girl?" Zack asked with a playful smirk.

"Well I am ready but with who ?" I asked laughing

"Real funny anna banana." He said as he pulled me closer from my waist.

Oops butterflies.

"Ooh you didn't just call me that Leslie." I said and stick my tongue out .

So since we were kids I hated when anyone called me anna banana as my grandfather used to tease me with that name. No one except him was allowed to call me that,well Zack didn't get it. So whenever he has to tease me. Where as Leslie is Zack's middle name no ine knows that, well we had made a pact that we won't let out these nicknames of ours and only use it for each other .

"So what are we gonna do today?" I asked.

"Well first I was gonna take you out on a date but then I remembered our little tradition." He said

"Oh my god! How could I forget our tradition!"

"So shall we?" He asked

"Let's bake something and totally ruin it!!" We screamed in unison and laughed .

"What should we bake?"he asked while going through the stuff thete was in out kitchen.

"Red velvet cake?" I suggested.

"Let's not get ahead of ourselves we aren't in MasterChef cupcake." He said and winked .

God tell him not to do this to me.

"What did you just call me?"

"Cupcake."

"OH YES! Let's make cupcakes!" I said and pecked him on the cheek. He smells like chocolate. Yum

" If you were gonna do that I would have suggest cupcake the first time ." He said and smirked

"Douche." I said and rolled my eyes.

"Wait anna." He said coming closer to me till I hit the kitchen counter and we were inches away from each other.

God is he gonna kiss me?

Yes!

No?

Yesss!

Oh my god.

I need help.

He slowly tucked my hair behind me ear,came closer to me. He came so close that there was almost no distance between us and whispered ,"well then you better tie up your hair anna banana or it will get dirty." And pulled my cheeks and smiled like a four year old.

This bitch!!

"You jerk you could have told me normally!" I said and slapped his arm

"It's not my fault you started imaging naughty things. " He said as jumped and sit on the kitchen counter while reading a recipe from the 'bake cakes' book mother had.

"Pervert." I said and gave him a stink eye.

"You imagining smut doesn't make me a pervert babe." He said as he took milk, eggs and flour out of the fridge

"Okay Leslie, let's make cupcakes." I said as I snatched the flour packet from his hands

"Easy there tiger . " He said

After a lot of trying we started mixing our cupcake batter and I pre heated the microwave as it was mentioned in the recipe. I saw Zack trying to eat the batter but I slapped his hand before he could eat it and he made the most adorable pouty face to which I squished his cheeks.

What a cutie this Jackass is.

Okay stop.

Still a cutie.

Ugh

Well after 30mins of bickering and trying to bake I put the batter in the cupcake thingies or whatever (a/n please forgive me I don't know a thing about baking)And I had a crazy idea.

I took some flour in my hand and said ,"hey Leslie look up here." He looked up and then immediately I threw the flour all over him and saw how funny he looked. Seriously he looked like the circus clowns it was difficult not to laugh at him

"Well well well anna, you brought yourself trouble babe." He said and took the entire packet of flour in his hands

God I did not see this coming! I gotta run

"No no no! Sorry sorry don't do this zackkkk!" I screamed as I ran to the living room

"Too late sav!" He said as he sprinted and ran towards me

Perks of being a jock.

Now I was on the top of the sofa with a fucking pillow as my shield and he had a packet of flour. God I don't wanna take a bath again please. We were circling each other like we were in a battlefield . Soon I tried to escape by running to my room but little did I know I am a stupid head.

As I was about to make a run he pulled me towards him as he circled his hands around my waist and pulled me back and practically shoved ke against the wall. At this point we both had heavy breathing tired of being on our fake battle. I looked at him and he smirked, he kept a gentle hand in my cheek as my hands rested in his neck. He pulled me closer till our breath tingled and our noses slightly touched he tilted his head and so did

I and he came closer till our lips were a few centimetres away and then our lips crashed.

32 - The First Date (part 2)

Zack's Pov

It was the most perfect kiss and the most perfect moment. It's been long since I had such strong feelings for anyone I had them for Brittany, I guess. I was just a hormonal Teenager at that time but with Anna it's so different, it's like every part of me knows it's right. I am too late for this, which I hate because I know she has feelings for kendall too, I can't do anything about it because well, feelings are feelings I was a jerk to her and I couldn't express what you felt for her it was obvious she liked Kendall from the first day they met in the bowling alley I saw how his eyes sparkled and i saw the look on Anna's face it's like she longed to see him, which made me feel weird. It bothered me since day one and to shake the feeling of liking my best friend I got back with Brittany that say, yes I am an asshole.

When I kissed her I could taste her strawberry lipbalm and she smelled like blue berries she must have used a new perfume which smelled really good. We were interrupted when we heard a smell of something burning.

Oh shit

"We burnt the cupcakes! God dammit!" She said as she face palmed herself.

"To be fair, it was kind of the goal so I could take my crush out on a date." I said as I held her hand.

"Oh who is she? Do I know her?" She asked.

God this girlllll!

"Nah you don't ,but she is like your twin."

"Oh where is my doppelganger then?" She asked while tapping her chin.

"Eh who cares, I will just take you out." I said as I winked at her and she blushed .

Adorable.

Heck I am turning into a girl

We cleaned the mess we had made and she changed into a new outfit and fixed her hair whereas I cleaned my self up and fixed my hair. When she came down I looked at her in awe, gosh she looked really pretty. She was wearing a red off shoulder dress which was hugging her body showing of her beautiful curves she perfectly did the messy hair thing and wore the necklace riley and I have her in her sweet sixteen.

"Are you done staring Leslie?" She asked with a smirk

"Yes ma'am , can we go know?" I said as took her hand in mine.

We thought of going to a restaurant nearby and have some food and then go for a movie , we sat in my car and talked the whole ride there was a bit of awkward silence but it didn't last long. We listened to our favourite songs bickered on who was better selena gomez or Miley Cyrus it was like the old times, when we hung out as best friends, it was different this time because it was a date .

Pov ends

Zack was a perfect gentleman, we went to the restaurant he ordered the food I always order. It was nice to see him pay attention to what I like or dislike, though it was pretty normal as he had known me for 11 years so even i remember his order at every food place by now I guess.

We ordered food, talk a lot, kid around a bit, flirted too and mostly teased each other. It has been long since Zack and I hung out like this. I forgot how good and light I felt with him . Ever since the feelings drama I knew I had missed my best friend in between which I didn't want to but now I felt I had my best friend back, just that we were on a date.

On the way back I was too tired for a movie so begged Zack to take me home. He was reluctant at first but then he suggested Netflix and chill. He said chill in a very flirtatious way to which I rolled my eyes. As we reached home I changed into Zack's sweatshirt and I noticed it smelled different, usually Zack's cologne smells like chocolate this smelled like lemon and green tea I know whose this is, I have smelled this before.

I went to my bedroom where Zack already had switched the tv on. Looking at me he said, " hey whose sweatshirt is that?" He asked

"I assumed it was yours" I replied.

"No it's not mine." He said whole shaking his head

Okay shit I know whose it is

It's kenny's!

How could I forget he left it here while he was leaving the other day.

Fuck Zack can't know!

"It must be one of dad's old sweatshirts." I said him. Lied to him

"Oh okay cool, so what do you wanna watch?"he asked.

"After we collided is out."I said

"I haven't seen the first part though." He said

"Well we'll watch both then." I said and gave him a big smile .

"As you wish m'lady." He said as he put his arm around me and tugged me closer to him which felt really good.

But the whole time I was with him I kept thinking any Kendall how I was wearing his hoodie when I was on a date with Zack. It seemed that the mere presence of Kendall's sweatshirt and occupied all my thoughts, I tried to drift away from them but I couldn't. I turned and looked at Zack. He gave a small peck on my forehead and I leaned on his shoulder.

What would kenny be doing right now? How will our date be tomorrow?

I was thinking all this and Zack realised it was already ten o'clock in the night and he had to leave as he has a match tomorrow even I was tired but today was perfect.

As he was about to leave he said ," Anna no matter who you choose I am always gonna be here as your best friend don't doubt that okay ? Well I would suggest you to choose me because well I am me and a bit selfish but I can't force you I know whatever decision you will make would be right." He gave me a reassuring smile and hugged me.

I was about to go to bed but before that I took a hot shower to think what all had happened today and what decision am I gonna make. With I these thoughts I drifted off to sleep excited for the day I was gonna spend with kenny tomorrow it would be our first official date. Soon i heard some noises like someone was out . I woke up to see someone was knocking at the window.

Is that Jesus?

Am I going to heaven?

What when did I die?!

I went and opened up my window and saw Kendall in my window who had climbed up to my window by stairs. What am I rupanzel? I was still a bit shocked about him showing up at my window at 4 am! Whoever knows me , knows that without proper sleep I am as good as a drug addict and I can be very dangerous and moody if I don't get my sleep.

I gave ken a 'why are you here in the fucking midnight look' and he said,

"Hey there, Juliet."

33 - The second date (part 1)

Kendall's Pov

It was a hard day knowing that savvy would be in a date with Zack . I was restless the whole day I couldn't think straight. All I wanted to do was make the next date for her perfect that's why I went to her house in the middle of the night . I know if she doesn't get her sleep she becomes very agitated, trust me you don't want to witness it but if this was probably the last day I would get to spend with her, I might as well make it worth it.

I took my car and went off to her house I knew exactly where to take her, the place was very special to us. It wasn't a palance or something but it was the place where Bianca the female protagonist of the movie 'The Duff' had her first kiss with Wes. It was the first movie she and I watched together and we both loved the movie. The special thing about the movie was the place it was full of greenery and was Bianca's secret safe spot,well the rock on that was. I was lucky to pin down the location of the place which was a few miles away from savvy's home. She said that she always wanted to be bianca to someone's Wes. Me being the lovesick puppy I was said

' I will be the Wes to your bianca.' she blushed when I had said that and god she looked adorable.

•~•~•

I pulled up in front of her house and climbed up to her window, I could see she was very frustrated as I had ruined her sleep. She came out and opened the window. She was wearing a hoodie with her hair open loose. She must have washed her hair .

"Hey there Juliet." I said and climbed up her window

"Okay what are you doing here? In the middle of the night?" She said in a low tone and muffles her hands into the oversized hoodie

Wait I is this my hoodie? Fuck this is my hoodie she is wearing!

Oh god seeing her in my clothes I couldn't help but scan her whole body she was wearing shorts underneath it and his those perfectly tanned legs. She looks hot..

"Hey eyes up here perv!" She said and raised her eyebrow.

"You are like riley 2.0 if someone disturbs your sleep princess." I said her expression changed as a call the princess and she was awkwardly blushing which I found very cute.

"I -- uh you still there answer my question what are you doing here in the middle of the night?"

"I want to take me somewhere get ready, I mean don't get your already in my clothes ." I said and winked at her.

"these are your clothes sorry I did not know I'm just gonna take it out and change." She said shyly.

"no no don't change your clothes just get a pair of leggings and come with me after taking somewhere . plus it's kind of good for me that you had your date with Zac and your wearing my clothes so I think it's a Win-Win . "

"You get over yourself." She said and laughed.

She put on a pair of leggings and help to get out of the window by the ladder. she hopped on in the car I need a pouty face I could figure out that she was still mad at me but I know I could make it up to her.

Pov ends

"Just question are you going to kidnap me ? " I asked which made ken chuckle a bit.

"well well now that i was planning on to kidnap you and take you away from zack as far as possible so that you did not have to make a decision ." He said.

"Well now aren't you wicked Kendall parker."

" Yes I surely am." He gave me a smirk which caused me to smile and then he drove off. To be very honest it felt really good to be out at night at this point of time . As the fresh air was coming over my face and I felt so free after such a long time and I felt relieved.

" Please tell me where are we going?" I begged him.

" Now princess it's a surprise tell you that the surprise won't be a surprise ."

"Pleaseeee" I made a puppy dog face.

"For the hundredth time I am not falling for this face ."

"Ughh fine have it your way. I have a question though." I asked.

"What is it?"

"you said that you are going to kidnap me but if I have feelings for zack instead of you then what would you do?"

"Well in that case I could just compel the guy to priesthood."

"ok you don't get to say that it's klaus's line."

" Oh did I offend your love of fictional life ?"

"You underestimating me and my loves of fictional life."

"Loves? How many are there ?and should I be concerned ?

"well the list starts with Damon Salvatore, klaus Mikealson, kol Mikealson ,Kai Parker and Lucas Scott and do you want me to go on kenny?" I said and gave him a smile.

"No you can stop your already hurting my ego . "

for the next 15-20 minutes we talked about random things and listened to songs. after a while we reach to the place I knew the place looks familiar but I just could not figure out where we were.

"Remember this?" He asked.

"Trying to but I still cannot get a hold of it."

"Well close your eyes till I get to the that spot ."

"Okay but ken I am trusting you here with my life."

" I promise not to break it, ever." He said as he came close to me ear which sent shivers down my spine and a faint smile appeared on my face.

He slowly made me walk through the woods and it was a while still be reached first I thought that we were lost but I trusted him enough to make sure I won't die today.

God help me. Is it too late to sing a prayer?

"Here we are." He siad and slowly removed his hand from my eyes.

Gosh

He brought me here?

To the Bianca and Wes spot?

He remembered it?!

Is this really true?

God this guy is the sweetest guy wish I could just kiss the life out if him right now.

Hey hormones, control.

"Y-- you remember the spot." I managed to say because I was still fascinated by the view.

"This is the place where Bianca and wes first kiss how could I forget this place was my first movie with you and I\promised to be the Wes to your Bianca one day ."

"This is the best thing that happened to me in such a long time oh my God I cannot thank you more." I squealed and jump into his arms.

He hugged me back and let out a sigh, like he was waiting for this to happen. I felt so safe in his arms. I took his scent in and he tightened his grip around my waist. I slowly pulled away and looked into his light brown eyes which managed to shine as the sun was coming up. That is when his lips came crashing down to mine.

It felt so different , my cheeks were heated up it was like sparks were in my body and there is no way to describe how I felt because I was so overwhelmed with these emotions. I couldn't think of any moment more perfect.

34 - Second date (part 2)

K endall and I weresitting on the rock waiting for the sunrise close the most beautiful place I have ever been in my entire life . Ever since I was a kid I always imagined to come here and look at the sunrise but I never knew that this place existed close to my house. visit there for about 2-3 hours and waited for the sun to come up while we were talking and reminiscing the days of the camp.

I was sitting there with my head on his shoulder and a fingers were entwined together that's when he asked , " wanna go back to my place for breakfast, princess?"

"It's our first date and you are already taking me to your home should I be scared? Wait what about my parents? They would be worries sick!" I said as I realised I had been away from my house since last night.

"You need to calm down I already told your parents that I would be stealing their daughter for the day ." He said and gave me a playful smirk.

" And you could not have told me this before when we were coming?"

"I wanted to see your freaking out look." He said and laughed off while I have him a light nudge.

We sat in his car and we drove up to his house when we reached everything was already on the breakfast table, scrambled eggs, bacon ,bread and mango juice. The perfect Idea of my breakfast or morning in general.

"Oh my god! You remember what I love to have for breakfast!!" I squealed and ran over to the food.

" Gosh woman, calm down!" He said and came after me.

"Geez I love you." I said

"What did you just say?" Ken said and gave me a startled yet blushing look.

God did I just say that?he must think I'm so weird I mean I have to cover this up oh my god think think savvy think .

"Ummm I meant-- uh bacon bacon,yes bacon I love it." I said and turned my face away.

Nice cover up! Way to go!

"Oh okay yeah bacon. Of course you love it." He said with a disappointed tone but still gave me a reassuring smile which made me very calm.

After we had the breakfast we switched on the TV we almost spent about 15 minutes on thinking what we have to watch but at the end we ended up watching Hannah Montana on Disney international. Okay it is not weird to watch Hannah Montana at the age of 17 it's fun when you sing along songs in a duet and run around the living room.

Gosh we are retarded kids.

"So what's the plan where are you going to take me next?" I asked and I slouched on the couch.

"Uhmm amusement park ." He said

"Oh what a good one." I said and laughed it off. He gave me a serious look when I realised that he wasn't joking.

"Oh my god no! No no no! You know I have a terrible fear od the rides there! I only go for the cotton candy! The Dorris wheel there scared the hell out of me! And the water rides you know I don't know how to swim! Kendall parker why would you take me there." I ranted all the way until I saw Kendall birat into fits of laughter.

"Look at you! You look so scared like you are about to get shot. Don't be sucha scaredy cat savvy! We have to go! I will be there, nothing is going to happen princess. " He said and cupped me cheek and kissed me forehead.

Opps butterflies again. Gosh I love this feeling.

"Igh fine ! But thisis a one time thing okay? Now Lemme get the clothes I packed and I am going to take a shower." I said and got up.

"Should I come with?" He said and traced my body with his eyes and nibbled his lip a bit. Gosh hot.

"No." I said and rushed to the washroom to hide the blush of my face.

After an hour or so we both got ready and left for the amusement park. Truth be told I was terrified to go but the idea of kendall with me somehow managed to calm my nerves down.

Throughout the drive we played Disney songs and jammed to it. We stopped at a signal with blasting music of high school musical and the car beside us had two teenage girls, who looked like twins,they rolled their windows down and jammed with us till the cars moved.

When we reached the amusement park it was like it was raided! It was filled with people who looked like they were having the time of their life . I let out a sigh because I had fear of rides but then ken held my hand and circled his thumb around and caressed my hand which made me feel like I was safe. I smiled at him and we went inside.

To be honest I think I was wrong about amusement parks after all. I mean it was the most fun day I was having. I felt so alive while I was in the rides . The excitement of the place screaming like no one was around you and laughing at all the crazy things ken and i were doing on the rides and at the food places.

I think I had a sugar problem after the three cotton candies I had. I swear they were the best thing I had eaten all day. I don't know if it was being with Kendall or the place that made me forget everything about the outside world all the worries, drama, tension that had been on my mind just disappeared. Being with kenny just had a different aura which I had never felt for a long time.

At last we went to the Ferris wheel I always had a feat of heights and this Ferris wheel was huge, like huge huge. We got on it and I had a feeling that something bad will happen and it did. We Fucking got stuck! On the top! I thought it only happened in movies. I started hyperventilating there was no stopping me now.

"Oh my god we are gonna die! I said that it was a bad idea! This Ferris wheel! What if we get stuck here? And we die and our corpses are the ones that fall off. Oh my god i don't wanna die!!"

"Hey hey savvy chill chill! You are gonna be fine, we are gonna be fine it would be a technical problem, Princess calm down." He said and came closer to me and caressed me back

"No no no technical problem can't be like this! I am telling we are gonna die we arw gon--" I was cut off when Kendall smashed his lips over mine.

It wasn't a soft,gentle kiss. It was a hot, passionate one. It was like we both longed for it to happen. I missed the feeling of him kissing me so I pulled him in closer and tugged his hair. His hands circled my waist and pulled me closer like till was no space between us. I forgot whatever was happening around me and it was like I was on cloud nine.

After a whole we separated and our foreheads were in contact as we breathed heavily. After a while the Ferris wheel started moving and I re-membered I freaked out I was a few minutes ago and now I even forgot that where i was with just one kiss.

Or one full on makeout sesh.

"We are moving." I said.

"I told you we are gonna be fine savvy." He said and pulled me closer so I could lean on his chest.

"I know with you everything is gonna be fine Kendall."

35 - Who is it?

It's been almost a week since I went out with Kenny and Zack. I have been having such a hard time deciding because I know I choose one I will lose another and I can't let that happen because both of them are equally important to me.

Its just that with both of them I feel differently, I like both of them in a different way I just can't decide who is the one . I mean how can I ever choose between them? One was my first crush and other was my first kiss. First kissed are always special, well if not special atleast it is something that a girl or guy would remember throughout their whole life.

Currently I was on my bed stuffing Oreos in my mouth like a hog because well, food held you in every life crisis and that's not wrong. As I was on my bed stuffing my face and eating my feeling the door bust open and riley appeared on the door .

"Wake up you sleepy ass!"

"God riles! You could have knocked."

"Have you met me anna?"

"Okay then, why are you here?"

"To help you choose between your playdates."

"I don't want to!"

"Hey listen to me Savannah lazy ass Orlove! I have been waiting for this day since Ken-doll came in town don't make me waitttt!" She squealed like a baby.

"So you want the tea?" I said and narrowed my eyes

"And ofcourse for your good it's a matter of life and death so chop,chop!"

"It's not that easy riley."

"Honey, I know it's not easy,that is why I am here ,okay? I know it will be difficult to choose but you had do to it someday and delaying won't help." She said with concern in here eyes.

I hugged her and said ," Thanks riley, it means a lot."

"Personally I prefer ken doll just so you know." She said and shrugged.

"You biased bitch." I said and threw a pillow at her and we both laughed

"So what do you think about the dates you spent with them how did you feel with each one of the two?" She asked.

I took a deep breath knowing that I had to let it all out it was now or never. So I started,

"Well with one I felt calm and comfortable like the day felt perfect and being with that person made me happy. Being with him made me realise how similar we are and how easy it is for me to be with him. The date was certainly very good and the time we spent together it was like the old days, the days I missed just hanging out and laughing , messing around without a care in the world like we had been friends forever."

"Okay though to beat but the another one?" She asked.

"The time I spent with the other one it was different like it was out of my comfort zone and rather than feeling pissed I felt amazing! It wasn't like a normal day for me it was out of the blue, I did something which I never expected to do because I am full of fears but being him just made them vanish. We had different interests and personality bit we still managed to get along very well. It was scaring yet exciting at the same time. I felt like I was complete and alive and even there was chaos around us, it didn't matter when I was with him." I said and sighed.

"Woah you actually beat the first one." She said and continued, " well I know who is who and I know what your choice should be but just what did you say how did it feel with the first one?" She asked.

"Calm and comfortable." I repeated

"No towards the end." She asked.

"Um like we have been friends forever?" I said .

"Do you realise what's wrong with it?" She asked me

"How can something be wrong with it?" I replied totally confused.

"Think Savannah!" She pressured.

"Just tell me already!" I shouted with curiosity in my voice

"It the word 'friend' , that is what is wrong with it." She said

"What do you mean?"

"Gosh anna! Do I have to draw you a map?"

"That would surely help riles." I said in a 'duh' tone.

"This whole date thingy wasn't for you to spend a day as friends! Or be or feel like you have been friends! It was for you to decide who you want to be with with the romantic feelings! It's not friends with benefits or you going to people and introducing the guy as ' hey look it's my boyfriend who is like a friend without feelings' ans stuff." She explained.

She has a very strong point

"What if i like the calm , friendly comfortable relationship more?" I asked.

"Relationships aren't supposed to always be calm and easy and sure as heck Not friendly! Relationships is about being involved romantically, not always being comfortable being uncomfortable yet in love and accepting your partner. Being different so that you don't ever run out of topics to talk about or things to do, keeping the excitement in the relationship . Relationships are never easy you have fights, disagreements which you have to overcome and make a relationship successful. By saying the things we are uncomfortable about makes the relationship with the person more comfortable."

"Woah. Relationship guru I am impressed." I said as I was recovering the lecture she threw on me.

"Okay fine leaving this, close your eyes and tell me the name that pops up when I say something." She said to which I agreed

"Okay so first going to a picnic."

"Kenny."

"Going horse riding."

"For sure kenny."

"Going bowling."

"Zack ."

"Romantic date."

"Kenny."

"Bunjee jumping."

"Ofcourse kenny ,Zack doesn't go one stuff like this."

"Going to a party"

"Zack."

"Going on a perfect proper date."

"It's ofcourse kenny."

Oh my god.

Oh my FREAKING GOD.

WHAT DID I JUST SAY?

"Look at that! Your subconscious and me both knew it was Ken-doll all along!" Riley screamed like a five year old who got three scoops of once cream.

'I -- how? I mean uh- Zack? What about him?" I said even though I was still shocked and unsure.

"Deep down even you know it has always been him, he was your first love and no one ever forgets their first love." She said.

"But Zack was my first kiss, I mean it's gotta mean something riley."

"Sweetie my first kiss was in the elevator with a guy who I used to think of as my brother but I didn't fall in love with him, I fell for Brian. Sure first kisses are important but your life doesn't depend on them. I don't even talk to the guy who was my first kiss it is just a memory in the back of my head that I won't forget but first love is something you never can keep as a back memory."

How could I not realise?

"All along it has been him."

It's always been kendall.

36 - It's You

Now that I had tbe courage to admit that Kendall is the one I want I was terrified what would happen to me and Zack and our friendship. I knew leading both of them on was a terrible idea but I had to tell the truth and first I had to go to zack because this can't be done on text or a call.

Riley went off on a date with Brian after our talk and trust me she skipped her way out of my room like she had found the guy she liked. It was like she was on cloud nine because of what I discovered and I was sitting myself into telling the truth.

I got out of the room and gathered up the courage and left to meet up zack at his house and took my car. I thought listening music would make me feel better which, well , always works but this time it didn't! God help me.

I reached at Zack's in 20 minutes. I was literally sweating my palms as I walked up to his house. My heart was palpitating, I was breathing heavily and thinking of the WORST case scenarios.

Ding dong.

I rang the doorbell and Zack opened the door with a warm smile and his face.

"Hey anna! Come inside, I haven't seen you in a week. "He said and hugged me

"He- hey- hi Zack."I said

"Are you okay? Come inside I will get you a soda or something."

"Yeah sure." I managed to take out those words.

As I sat on his couch he left for his kitchen when I heard Sherlock Holmes ringtone.

God am I in a crime scene?

What I am doing is this bad?

Why is this music playing in my head?

I looked down and saw my phone vibrating

Oh yeah it's my ringtone.

WAIT.

WHY IS KENDALL CALLING?

NO NO NO NO.

Can my life be more fucked?

I picked up the phone with a brave heart not trying to think what is the worst thing he could even say to me not like he knows I made a decision.

"Hey kennnyyy! Whaddup my man?" I said and then cringed at my own words

Real smooth.

"Hey savvy, I just called because riley called me and said you made your decision about the dates and all so I just wanted to ask you, have you?"

Oh he does know.

Well it could not get any worse than this right?

"So you came here to tell me that I am the one you chose and not Kendall?" Zack said from the kitchen, well practically shouted

Oh it does get worse.

God this is the right time to bless me.

I am sorry I picked up a candy that was fallen on the ground but I think we compromised that it was under 5 seconds!

"Are you with Zack?" Kendall asked.

"I-- um it's just ken- you know-" but I was cut off

"Why are you on the phone when you came here to declare your undying love for me anna?" Zack said when he was in front of me

"So it is Zack, I should have known. I am sorry to talk your time. Good bye Savannah." Ken said and cut the call.

Did he just call me SAVANNAH?

God no no no.

"Zack in I came here to tell that."

"It's not me who you chose right?" He finished my sentence.

"Huh? What?" I asked him in confusion.

"Well because the way you come in I know it wasn't a good news, I know when you are scared to admit a thing you start fidgeting."

"Zack I am so sor--".

"No I haven't finished yet anna."

Oh god lord he hates me.

"I don't hate you anna."

Is he a mind reader?

"It's just that I think I always knew in my heart that you would choose kendall. I mean since he came Into town you have a different glow on your face you aren't stuck up instead you are free and happier like a more alive version of yourself. Plus when did exactly you have feelings for me?" Zack asked.

"After that dare where we had to kiss." I said

"Yes which I said wasn't a big deal but after that even a thing we did as best friends seemed like you were having second thoughts because I was your first kiss. I know how hyped up you were always about your first kiss. Not just you, even me. Ever since we kissed there was some tension between us which we took as feelings but no they weren't romantic feelings I think we both know that."

"When did you get so wise?" I asked him.

"I always have been I just never showed it because you were my best friend who always figured out stuff. Yes I do like you yes it would hurt me to see you with him but I want you to be happy and well the heart wants what it wants right?"

"Yes it does but are we good? You aren't mad at me?"

"No sav, you are my best friend you will always be my best friend and I am always here for you, I want you to do the same, can you?"

"Be your best friend and tolerate you for my whole life? Sounds questionable." I said and looked at him and he laughed a little

"Yes Zachary Leslie Ryder. I am and always be your best friend it will be an honor."

"Well it should be Savannah Pemberton Orlove, now get that golden boy of yours."

I got on my toes,kissed him on the cheeks and sprinted my way as one thing was over.

"Have fun, not too much okay? But still use protection anyway." he said as I made a way to the door

"I will mommmmm!" I shouted back.

Mission- let's get to Kendall

I was in a good mood finally well because Zack and I were still best friends and one tension was over but then I remembered the call with kendall.

Oh gosh I hope I reach in time.

I reached at his house and saw his door was open and a suitcase was already out.

Okay no no this isn't happening.

I rushed inside and literally sprinted up the stairs to Kenny's room where he was packing his stuff and was clearly not in a good mood.

"Kendall hey." I said and he turned around with a sad expression..

"Look if you came here to say goodbye, don't. I gotta go." He said and looked away.

"No please listen to me." I said as I took a step further towards him.

"What? What is there left to listen,huh? A crappy apology? Or why you chose Zack instead of me? Or you want us to be friends? Please Savannah there is nothing you can say to stop me. You made your decision I made mine." He said and stormed off to the door.

"It's you Kendall, not Zack or not any other guy in this whole world." I said with all the energy I had.

"What?" He turned around and looked me with disbelief.

"It's you Kendall, I went to zack's to tell him that it's not him that I wanna be with, it's not him I am crazy about, it's not him.who I had a crush since I know boys don't have cooties, it's not him I see a future with and most importantly it's not him I am in love with."

" oh my god-- are you, is this, is this really happening?"

"Yes, I am sorry that I took so long to-" it was then that I was cut off by him as he rushed towards me pulled me closer and smashed his lips on mine.

Gosh I love this feeling.

After a while he pulled away as his hand cupped my face and he had tears in his eyes and looked me with his gentle brown eyes of his filled with love.

"I can't believe this is true." I said.

"It is savvy, and it is in this moment that I tell you what I have always wanted to."

"And what is that ken?"

"I love you, Savannah Orlove."

"I love you too, Kendall parker."

Maybe this is the start of our always and forever.

~The end ~